OUT OF HAND

A DC O'Connell Thriller
Book 3

By
A L Fraine

The book is Copyright © to Creative Edge Studios Ltd, 2020.
No part of this book may be reproduced without prior permission of the copyright holder.

All locations, events, and characters within this book are either fictitious, or have been fictionalised for the purposes of this book.

Book List

The complete A L Fraine Book list:
www.alfraineauthor.co.uk

Table of Contents

Book List 2
Table of Contents 3
Acknowledgements 4
Chapter 1 5
Chapter 2 11
Chapter 3 17
Chapter 4 18
Chapter 5 25
Chapter 6 31
Chapter 7 36
Chapter 8 43
Chapter 9 46
Chapter 10 51
Chapter 11 59
Chapter 12 65
Chapter 13 72
Chapter 14 78
Chapter 15 82
Chapter 16 88
Chapter 17 92
Chapter 18 95
Chapter 19 100
Chapter 20 109
Chapter 21 114
Chapter 22 119
Chapter 23 124
Chapter 24 131
Chapter 25 145
Author Note 149

Acknowledgements

Thank you to my wife and family for all your support and for believing in me. I love you all.

Thank you to my proofreaders for your help.

Thank you to Hanna Elizabeth, my Editor, for her hard work.

Thank you to Barry Hutchison, for being a great sounding board in this process.

Thank you to Surrey Police for their time and help.

Thank you to my readers, because without you, none of this would be possible.

Enjoy.

Note:
This book is written in British English.

Chapter 1

"So, what would you like to do first, hmmm?" the young lady said to him as she walked through his entrance hall, her heels clicking on the marble floor. She ran a finger along the top of a table as she admired the décor, and came to a mirror. She glanced over at him, twisting her slender body as she moved, letting him enjoy the shape of her.

She smiled and turned, bending over and checking her makeup in the mirror.

Alister's eyes wandered to the escort's rear, and although she was not the one he'd ordered, she would be a worthy replacement. He enjoyed the ripple of the girl's muscles in her legs as she went up onto her tiptoes to get closer to the mirror.

"So, um, Mindy was it?"

"Mmm-hmm," Mindy replied as she finished reapplying her ruby lipstick, and dropped it in her bag. She turned and put her butt to the table edge, lifting one foot off the floor to rub it up the back of her other calf.

She bit her lip and smiled.

"Did Shelly tell you what we usually do?"

"No, sorry. We didn't get time to talk before I left. Nothing *too* naughty, I hope," she teased.

The way she said those words, so full of hidden meaning and secrets, sent his pulse racing. He approached her, wanting nothing more than to lift her dress and take her right there against the table. He could already feel himself getting aroused by her and the unvoiced promises she was hinting at.

She glanced down and then back up to his eyes. "Getting excited, are we?" She cocked an eyebrow at him.

"I guess," he replied and stepped closer, placing his hands on her hips and running them up over her sides, feeling her warmth as he pressed his pelvis into her.

"Oh, my word, Mr Langley. Feeling frisky, are we?"

She seemed almost reluctant as he leaned in and kissed her neck. She placed her hands on his rear and pulled him in close and he forgot his doubts. He enjoyed the feel of her pressing against him as he caught his reflection in the mirror.

He sometimes wondered what these girls really thought of him—a man in his fifties, hiring them each week to satisfy himself. He paid them well and always treated them with kindness and respect, but they both knew they were here for one thing, and one thing only.

"Oooh, what's that?" she asked and slipped sideways, stepping away from him. She pulled her dress back down over her hips as she walked towards the modern glass door and walls. "Is that a library?"

Alister blinked and sighed. She wasn't the first person, or escort, to comment on what was behind that door. The stacks were well lit and filled with carefully placed volumes, many of them ancient and delicate.

Mindy walked right up to the locked door and pressed her hands against it as she peered through.

"That's amazing."

Alister smiled. "Thank you."

"Can I have a look?"

Alister walked up behind her, reached up and gently took hold of her slender wrist, removing her hand from the glass. He frowned at the greasy mark her hand had left on the door.

He'd have to clean that later.

"Maybe afterwards," he answered, feeling annoyed by the distraction.

Mindy looked up at him, her eyes pleading. "Oh, please? I love books. Their feel, their smell. Hmmm," she purred. "Helps get me in the mood."

Alister stared at her for a moment. Was she being serious? Looking at books turned her on? "I can think of other things that might do that for you."

Mindy pressed into him again, her hand on his chest. "You wouldn't deny me just a little peek..." Her hand slid south, over his body and slipped into the front of his slacks where she wrapped her exploring fingers around him. "…would you?"

Alister closed his eyes for a moment and enjoyed the feel of her fingers running over him, visualising all the things he could do with her.

"Please?" she pressed once more.

"Okay, okay. You can have a quick look, but you mustn't touch anything, do you understand?"

She gave him a playful squeeze and then withdrew her hand with a wink. "Guide's honour."

Alister wanted this over and done with quickly. He moved to the security keypad and quickly keyed in the code.

Between the layers of ballistic glass, the metal locking mechanism withdrew and the indicator light turned green as air hissed through the seals.

"Wow," Mindy said.

"It's a sealed, temperature and humidity-controlled room, it helps keep the books in top condition."

"Must have cost you a lot to get installed."

"Yes, but it's worth it," he said as he turned the handle and swung the door wide. Mindy stepped into the room right away. Alister swallowed nervously as she took a few steps between the stacks. He watched intently, minding where her hands went, but she kept them close and didn't reach out.

She pointed to a nearby volume on the shelf before her. "What's this?"

Alister frowned and stepped into the room, unable to see what she was looking at from where he was. "I, um… Err…"

"They're all beautiful. This is an incredible collection. What are they about?"

"Various esoteric subjects," he replied, preferring to keep things vague, lest he scare her off.

She turned her head slightly and gave him a lop-sided smile. "The occult?"

"Um… Yes. Some."

"You dirty dog."

Alister raised an eyebrow at her comment.

"Who would have thought it? A nice old man like you with an occult library in the heart of Surrey. My, you are a contradiction. I had no idea that was what you were like."

"Like?"

"You're a bit of a black sheep, aren't you?"

"No less than yourself."

The girl smiled. "You have no idea."

Pain exploded on the back of Alister's head. He dropped to the floor with a grunt and reached up to feel where he'd been struck. The world swam, and he struggled to make much sense of what he was seeing.

Dark shapes loomed above him.

"You took your time," a woman said. Was that Mindy speaking?

"All good things, my dear, all good things."

"I had to touch his wrinkly dick to get him to open this door."

"And it's a sacrifice I'm eternally grateful for," replied the man.

"Yeah," replied another. "You make a fucking hot whore."

"Piss off, before I rip your cock off," Mindy replied.

"Indeed, a little respect please," the first man replied.

"Sorry, boss."

As his vision began to clear, he felt himself being sat up against something.

"Hello? Anyone in there? I didn't hit you that hard."

Alister blinked and looked up at the face of the bald man before him. He was a mountain, with broad shoulders and a rugged face.

"You in there?" he asked.

"Wha… What do you want?" Alister asked as he tried to focus on his predicament and not the throbbing lump that was growing on the back of his skull.

"Ah, he speaks. Welcome back, old man. Well, the answer to that is simple. We want a book."

"I have many, take one," he moaned, just wanting them out.

"A very specific book," the thug replied.

It was a struggle, but Alister managed to lift an eyebrow and look up at the man as he stood up straight.

"I have your attention now, do I?"

"Which book?" Alister asked. He had many in here, and while all of them were precious to him and he desperately didn't want to lose any of them, he'd still put the value of his own life above any of them.

Well… almost any.

"Oh, this isn't just any book. This is a special book. A very special book."

"I have many books in here that are important to me," Alister replied, unable to narrow it down to a single volume.

"I believe it goes by the name of Liber Exterious."

"Oh…" Alister replied, suddenly aware of just what the man was talking about.

"Yes."

"That book."

"Indeed."

"Well, I'm afraid you're out of luck. I don't have it," Alister replied truthfully. He didn't have it. Not here, anyway, and he'd rather die than let these guys get it.

"Really?" the man replied.

"Really."

"Well, that is a shame," the man answered and turned away. Alister couldn't see what he was doing. After a moment, the man pulled his shirt off, revealing the huge tattoo that covered his back.

It was a fierce-looking, intricately designed dragon that covered his entire back. The man spread his arms wide in sinuous lines as if he was a dancer playing to a crowd, his muscles bulging.

"I am the Dragon. I am strength and fire, and I will not be denied."

One of the other men approached, Alister could see at least two others besides the one who called himself Dragon and Mindy, but there could be more out of view. The thug held up a wooden box for the Dragon, who turned to it and opened it reverentially. He withdrew a pair of gleaming, ornate daggers, and held one in each hand before turning to face Alister.

"Talk, or don't," the Dragon replied. "We'll find it either way." He moved in a blur, and a deep screaming pain exploded in Alister's gut as the Dragon plunged a knife into him. "Your sacrifice will not be in vain."

Chapter 2

Kate closed the door of the small dishwasher in her kitchenette and checked the time. It was still a little early. She didn't like to be the first one at these resident meetings, lest she get grilled by Francine.

She shook her head and sighed. She meant well, but she was a product of her generation in many ways.

The dynamic at these meetings had changed since they'd found out Kate was a detective, and she felt sure they were slightly on edge around her. Always watching what they were saying.

It was both amusing and annoying in equal measure.

Crossing her apartment, she approached her small desk and caught sight of the letter she'd pinned up just a few short weeks ago.

The small slip of white paper had two short sentences on it.

No more letters. Let the games begin.

A feeling of recurring dread manifested each time she looked at it, and tonight was no different. It was the letter that the man claiming to be her aunt's killer had given her from the depths of his shadowy car. But since that day, nothing had happened that she could pin on him. No more letters. Nothing.

She'd been on edge about it ever since that meeting, wondering when he'd suddenly pop out of the shadows to mess with her. Would he'd try to kill her, too? He probably knew that Kate and her Aunt had been close. Did he think she'd said something to Kate? Something incriminating? Something important?

Kate looked away and sighed. She hated this, she hated the waiting. Part of her just wanted him to get on with whatever sick and twisted plan he was going to carry out so she could hunt him down and put him behind bars.

But given that he'd killed already and showed no remorse for it, she also didn't want him to return to his bad habits. She'd take taunting letters over dead bodies, any day.

As she stood and looked at nothing in particular, she heard a door go in the corridor outside. That was one of her neighbours heading downstairs for the meeting.

They were fairly pointless affairs, discussing which lightbulb they were going to replace this week or some other pointless thing. She didn't care. She had bigger things to worry about, but she also knew she needed to attend when she was around. It didn't send a good message about the dedication of the police if she never went to them. Besides, she worked late often enough that she only attended one out of three.

Grabbing her keys, she stepped outside and locked her door.

"Good evening," said a voice from nearby.

Kate looked up and smiled at Clyde, one of the three other people who lived up here in the smaller apartments. He was the second-oldest in the building after Francine, and a friendly man with a local accent.

"Evenin'," Kate replied with a smile, turning to face him. The upstairs landing was just a short stretch of corridor at the top of the stairs with the four doors leading off of it to the apartments. "Another meeting."

"Indeed. Francine enjoys them, I think. It's always nice to have something to focus on later in life. Trust me on this."

Kate smiled. "I can understand that.

"Busy week, detective?"

"They're always busy weeks," she replied reflecting on the smaller, simpler murder cases she'd been involved with since wrapping up the Solomon case. There was always something to work on, but the involvement of the National Crime Agency had changed things for Nathan and herself somewhat. They were still assigned cases, but their new priority was working on looking into the conspiracy behind the Solomon and Wilson murder sprees, and the organisation that Inspector Damon Verner said was named the Black Hand.

Not that this had been an easy task. There were far more dead ends than there were breakthroughs. It was almost as if the organisation didn't exist, and there were times when Kate almost believed that this was the case.

Were they chasing a red herring?

And yet, both she and Nathan were sure that something bigger was going on. There were some clear links and similarities between the two cases, and some less obvious ones too, but proving these things and making them fit together for a court of law, would be tricky.

Then, there was the extra training that Damon had insisted on. She had to admit, it was cool, but part of her wondered if it was truly needed.

"It's like they say, no rest for the wicked," Clyde replied.

"Indeed. What about you? Have you been busy?"

"You'd think that being retired would mean I'd have more time to myself, but I'm finding that incredibly, I almost have less. Or, it certainly feels that way, at least. You know, visiting friends, playing golf. I'm rarely bored."

"The life of a bachelor," Kate quipped as they made their way downstairs. "Sounds like it's a hard one."

"Torturous," Clyde answered as a door opened behind them.

Kate looked up to see Monika step out of her flat and follow them downstairs. "Oh, this is good, I not late," said in her Polish-accented English

Kate smiled. "No, not yet."

"Don't ever be late," Clyde added.

"No. Mrs Hershey not like that, at all," Monika replied. "Good to see you here for meeting, Kate."

"Thanks. It feels like it's been a while."

"You busting bad guys. Makes you very busy."

Kate smiled at Monika. "It can do."

"I notice you always get pass from Mrs Hershey when you not come to meetings."

"She's a detective," Clyde replied and leaned in towards Monika. "That means she's respectable, unlike the rest of us reprobates."

Monika looked confused. "Rep-oh-bate? I do not know this word, but I guess it mean not worthy person?"

"Close enough," Kate answered. "Now, shhh," she instructed them as she knocked on the door to Francine's ground floor flat. She could hear talking inside, and seconds later, the door opened.

"You're here! Kate! It's so lovely to see you again," Francine said clearly thrilled, and guided her inside. "Clyde, Monika, come in, come in." She didn't sound quite as excited to see them.

Aziz from upstairs and Jaida from across the hall were both here, both full of smiles as Kate walked over. "Evening. You alright?"

"Yeah," Aziz replied.

"Ed's looking after the kids so, yeah, of course," Jaida answered. "Good timing, by the way. I think having two non-whites in her home was stressing Francine out."

Kate laughed.

"She seemed very pleased to see you," Aziz added.

"Of course," Jaida commented. "Kate's whiter than she is and has a respectable job in her eyes."

"Hey! I know I'm pasty but…"

"Practically ghost-like," Jaida replied with a wink.

"Heh, thanks for that. But you have respectable jobs, too," Kate protested. "I bet most of you earn more than I do."

"You're a police officer. Of course, we earn more than you do," Jaida snarked.

"Jaida has a respectable job," Aziz replied. "At least Francine understands what a teacher is."

"Which no doubt messes with her head," Jaida agreed with a smile. "A black woman teaching kids? Whatever's next!"

Aziz laughed. Kate glanced back to make sure Francine wasn't listening in, but she was talking with Clyde. They weren't being serious and just having fun, but it was clear to

Kate that on many occasions Francine's bias, conscious or unconscious, coloured her actions. She didn't hate people with dark skin, she just held certain beliefs and ideas that she'd been working through in recent years. She'd come a long way, but it remained a frequent talking point between some of her flatmates.

"Yeah. But I work in IT, which might as well be witchcraft as far as she's concerned." He pointed to one of several crosses mounted to the walls.

"You're being a little harsh," Kate moderated.

"Oh, don't get us wrong," Jaida replied. "She's lovely. I like her, I do. But she is a product of her generation."

Kate nodded, smiling. She couldn't argue with that. Francine's ginger tom-cat, Jethro, bumped into her leg. "Oh, hey there, fella," she said and bent down to pet him. He purred affectionately as she stroked him, before getting bored and wandering off.

"Anyone want a drink?" Francine asked as she approached, now that Clyde had finally let her go.

"I won't say no," Kate answered.

"What would you like, dear?" Francine was easily over sixty, and it showed. But she was a kind lady who wanted to make sure everyone in the building got along and did as the new landlord asked, now that Wilson Hollins was no longer the owner of the building. "Tea, coffee?"

Kate felt like asking for a glass of wine and thought longingly about the bottle she knew she had in the fridge upstairs. "A coffee would be lovely, thank you."

"Of course, dear. I'll be right back."

"She's really taken to this idea of being the building's de facto leader," Clyde commented when Francine was out of earshot.

"She loves it," Kate agreed.

"What do you think of the new landlord? We hardly see him."

"He's better than Mr Hollins was," Aziz answered.

"Yeah," Kate replied, thinking back to her first case on the Surrey Murder Team.

"Did they pull out all the cameras in your flat?"

"They did," Kate answered.

"That was messed up," Jaida stated.

"You're not wrong." She remembered seeing her apartment on that monitor in the commercial unit, and everything else she'd found in that particular house of horrors, and a shiver ran up her spine.

"Did he go to prison?"

"They're still not done with the court case, but he's being held in custody for now, yes."

"They're not done?" Aziz replied.

"They take a while to complete, and he's got a good lawyer so…"

"I hope justice prevails," Jaida said.

"Me too," Kate agreed. "Me too."

Chapter 3

He sat himself down at the computer and sighed. It had been another long day, but his plans were finally coming to fruition. He'd find out how the raid went soon enough and kept his fingers crossed for some good news.

Time would tell on that particular front. In the meantime, several other things would start to happen over the next few days and he couldn't wait to see how Kate would react.

That would be the particularly delicious part of all this.

He eyed the envelope on the table beside him, knowing what was inside, and smiled to himself before returning his attention to the computer screen. For a moment, he sat there, wondering how long he should wait before heading over there.

No, it's too early, and I could do with a little light relief.

He tapped the mouse and the computer screen flared into life.

Quickly, he navigated through the folders until he found what he was looking for and opened up the directory.

Inside, row after row of video clips were lined up in order of date created, but he clicked on through into another folder labelled Favourites.

There were fewer videos in this folder, but they were the best ones. The real cream of the crop. Standing up, he undid his belt and lowered his trousers before sitting and touching himself as he considered which video he wanted to watch. Making his choice, he double-clicked one of them. HD footage of the inside of an apartment appeared, complete with a naked Kate on her bed.

The man smiled and hit play. Sitting back, he took hold of himself and began to enjoy the view.

Chapter 4

Sitting on the edge of her bed, Kate wiped her eyes and blinked at the shaft of light that streamed in through the gap in the curtains. It splashed across the floor and bounced around her apartment.

She yawned, stretched, and then spotted the envelope on the floor near the door.

She froze.

"Shit." Standing up, wrapping her arms around herself, she looked around her flat to see if anything else was out of place or different, but there was nothing. Just that innocuous-looking envelope on the floor that called to her, beckoning her to pick it up and open it.

She stepped over and crouched down beside it. It had the usual, familiar handwriting she'd come to know so well from all the other letters her aunt's killer had sent her, and her stomach sank.

Was this the start? Was this the day that the killer would make his move?

She picked up the letter and sat at her desk where she quickly ripped it open to find a single printed photo inside.

She stared at the image for a long moment, recognising the man in the wheelchair with the vacant expression on his face.

Scrawled across it in sharpie two words were written:

I know.

Kate dropped the photo on her desk and sighed. She didn't have time for this. She had another long day at work ahead and she couldn't spend her day worrying about what this idiot might do to her.

Kate left the photo where it was, and quickly got showered and dressed before grabbing a slice of toast and heading out the door. As usual, she was probably the first up in the building, so she crept out of her door and set off down the stairs, only to freeze partway down.

At the bottom of the stairs, on the floor outside Francine's flat, lay her cat, Jethro on his back. Dead. Its ginger fur was covered in deep, dark red splatters, and the animal wasn't moving.

"Shit," Kate cursed, and moved down the steps as quietly as she could, peering up the short corridor to the front door, and back the other way to the rear door that led into the communal garden. She was alone.

She could smell it as she approached, and noticed a slip of paper that had been stapled to the poor thing.

She inclined her head, trying not to look at the exposed innards of the dead animal. The same familiar writing that was on her letter was on the note here too, and once again, there were just two words.

From Kate.

"Bastard," Kate hissed as sudden understanding washed over her. He was trying to turn her flatmates against her.

Reaching down, she grabbed the note and ripped it off. It came away easily. She screwed it up and stuffed it in her pocket, before sighing and sliding the doormat the cat was laid upon to one side so Francine wouldn't see it right away. Satisfied, Kate pressed the buzzer on Francine's door.

She couldn't just leave Jethro there. Jaida's kids would be leaving soon to head out for school. It needed to be moved before they saw it. Spotting a discarded plastic bag nearby, Kate grabbed it and laid it over the grisly wound on the cat's belly. Francine needed to know what had happened, but there was no need for her to see cat's insides.

Kate heard approaching footsteps inside the flat and braced herself. She wouldn't admit to knowing who'd done it. That would be ridiculous and spark more questions than it answered.

She'd say it was random thugs. No, a car accident. That was better.

The lock on the door turned.

***

"How was the meeting?" Nathan asked from his desk, a short distance away.

"Yeah, alright," Kate answered. "You know, the usual." The events of the morning had left Kate more than a little shell-shocked. Francine had been upset by the death of her cat, understandably so, and Kate offered to take care of it for her, for which Francine was extremely grateful.

Francine accepted her explanation of Jethro being hit by a car, and Kate had then spent the next forty-five minutes digging a shallow grave for him in the back garden and then standing with Francine as she said a few words.

Luckily, only Clyde saw them quietly burying the cat. He came out to comfort Francine as Kate covered over the cardboard box they'd used in dirt. She was at least glad that Jaida's kids hadn't seen it.

As Kate had dug the grave, she wondered what the killer thought he was doing. Was he watching this, somehow? Was he laughing at them, enjoying the torment he was causing?

"I only ask because you were late in today," Nathan said, staring at her.

"Oh, yeah. Sorry. Got a little held up at the flat, and then hit some traffic." It wasn't a total lie.

"Sure thing. I just thought you'd be in early today, you know?"

"Early?"

"We get them today, remember?"

Kate looked blankly at her partner, her mind scrambling to catch up until she suddenly remembered. "Oh, yeah. Damn, I forgot about that."

"I think Sam's jealous," Nathan remarked.

"I bet he is," Kate agreed as she looked up to see DCI Malcolm Dean wander over to them. He stopped a few feet away and shoved his hands in his pockets with a grumpy sigh.

"Right then, let's get this over with, shall we?"

"You're coming with us?" Kate asked.

"Aye. I don't agree with this, but the orders came from higher up."

Kate nodded. DCI Dean had made his feelings clear about their new training from day one, and in many ways, Kate agreed. It felt kind of unnatural, for here in the UK. But times were changing, and images of recent terror attacks and the responding officers that were on-scene played out in her mind, showing her that it wasn't as uncommon as you'd think.

"This isn't the United States, and I don't believe that Detectives in this country should be armed as a matter of routine," the DCI finished.

Kate shrugged. "I agree. We shouldn't. It sets a precedent, and not a good one."

DCI Dean agreed with a curt nod.

"This isn't our call, though," Nathan replied. "And after seeing what the followers of this Black Hand are capable of, I know I would feel much safer going after them armed."

"I know," the DCI said, his tone resigned. "I've spoken with Damon and Chief Superintendent Collins about this many times, and they're both adamant on this point."

Kate nodded again. After going through an intensive training course on firearms, she felt confident and at ease with them, and she had to agree with Nathan when it came to the major killers they'd taken on recently. These were not your usual crimes, and special crimes required special measures. As AFOs—Authorised Firearms Officers—she and Nathan were now a part of a special operational unit working closely with the NCA on the Black Hand case.

"Is Sam jealous?" Nathan asked, glancing over at the DI.

"Livid," the DCI answered with a smile.

"Excellent."

"Right, come on. Move your asses. I've not got all day."

Kate jumped up and walked with Nathan and Malcolm through the office. Stepping into the stairwell, they made their way down to the rear ground floor of the building, close to where the station's armed officers were based. The DCI led them into the armoury, where first Nathan, and then she was issued a Glock 19M and three magazines of ammunition, which they both took time to secure to their persons via the shoulder holsters they had been issued.

It felt a little odd and bulky to wear when she first put it on, but she knew from experience over the last few weeks, she soon forgot about it.

"Well, congratulations," DCI Dean said as Kate turned back him. "Try not to kill anyone, won't you?"

"Of course, sir," Nathan replied. Kate considered a flippant response, but decided against it, given the circumstances.

"Right, go on then, off you go."

Kate nodded and followed Nathan out of the armoury and back upstairs. As she walked through the various areas that she passed through every day, she felt very aware of what was under her jacket.

It felt odd to just wander around carrying a loaded gun as if it were nothing. But she also knew they had been authorised to do so for a very specific purpose.

"Does it feel off to you?" Kate asked.

Nathan nodded. "It feels a little strange, but I'm sure we'll get used to it."

"Yeah. I guess. I hope I don't have to use it."

"Don't jinx yourself like that."

"Ooops," Kate replied.

"You'll be gunning down bad guys by next week now," Nathan joked as they walked back into the main office.

"Hey, look, it's Bonnie and Clyde," DI Sam Mason called out as they passed.

"Do you want to hold it?" Kate replied with a smirk. "Would it make you feel more like a man?"

"Do you feel more like a man?" Sam said, with one raised eyebrow.

"I did ask for a Hello Kitty-branded one, but alas..." Kate answered with a shrug.

"Shame."

"They might have a Power Rangers one for you though, if you could pass the course."

"Fat chance of that," Nathan added.

Debby Constable, one of the desk clerks strode over to them. "Chief Superintendent Collins would like to see you both."

"Okay, thanks Deb," Nathan answered, and led the way through the station to the Chief's office.

"Come in, come in," he said as they arrived. "Well done on passing the course. You did well."

"Thank you, sir," they both answered.

"You know why you've been asked to do this, don't you?"

"We do, sir," Nathan replied.

"Damon and I have spoken at length about this. He suggested that you be armed now that you're a Special Operational Unit. Damon has made me aware of some of the history of the Black Hand organisation, and some of the things they have supposedly been involved in. They're one of several organisations that have cropped up as being behind various crimes over the years, both here and internationally, but it's only recently that Damon, with the help of various security services, has linked many of those events together. Clearly, he thinks you are both valuable in this fight, which is why you have been tasked with this mission. Damon will be working closely with you from here on out, so treat him as one of the team."

"We already do, sir," Kate replied. "We've been through much of the research that he's compiled over the years, and if even five percent of his conclusions are right, then we're clearly dealing with a powerful and insidious group."

"They do seem to have hit some setbacks recently, though," Nathan continued. "They seem to have shrunk, and are keeping their more recent activities to the British Isles, primarily around London and the home counties."

"Well, he's made it clear to me that you are both valuable assets in the fight," the Chief replied. "The fact that he's chosen you to help, makes me proud to have you on my team, for however long that turns out to be…"

"Oh?" Nathan asked. "Something up, sir?"

"Hopefully it's nothing, but I've had word that the Chief Constable is currently reconsidering the viability of the Horsley Station. It's mainly a cost issue. The Surrey Constabulary's budget is stretched thin enough already, and running a station like this, out here in the countryside, is perhaps not the best use of funds. So, I don't know... I guess we'll see what happens."

"So the station might be shut down?" Kate asked.

"Possibly," the Chief Superintendent replied.

"Christ..."

Nathan's phone rang. He pulled it from his pocket and looked at the caller ID. "Sorry sir, I think we need to take this."

"Of course, go on. Don't let me keep you."

Kate watched Nathan take the call as she followed him out of the office. He wasn't on long before he ended the call and looked at Kate. "That was Damon, he thinks he has a case for us."

Chapter 5

"Here we are," Kate announced as she spotted several patrol cars parked up along the side of the road on either side of a driveway. Nathan pulled in onto the gravel drive where a uniformed officer held up a hand for them to a stop just short of a large wooden gate set between two pillars.

The officer checked their ID before letting them through.

The house beyond was an impressive, modern affair. Large and well looked-after with recently mown lawns and flower beds that didn't have a single weed in them.

The sight was marred slightly by the collection of police vehicles that had congregated in the driveway.

Nathan pulled off to one side onto the lawn, leaving enough space for others to get out.

"Another wealthy victim," Kate remarked as she climbed out of the vehicle.

"Money seems to have that effect, doesn't it?" Nathan agreed.

"You mean, it paints a target on your back?"

Nathan smiled. "Yeah, something like that," he said and led the way over the driveway to the house. Kate kept her ID to hand and flashed it at a couple of officers who approached them and then directed them inside.

"Ahh, about time you two got here," Constable Louis Dyson said with a smile as he walked up. You pair always get the gruesome ones."

"That bad, is it?" Kate asked.

"He's been gutted like a fish," Luis replied.

"Thanks for that," Kate replied, grimacing.

"Who's here?" Nathan asked.

"The usual. Sheridan's in there leading the investigation. I think your boss is on his way."

"DCI Dean?"

"That's him," Luis confirmed. "There's a weird guy in there, too. Inspector Verner or something? Something to do with the National Crime Agency."

"We know him," Nathan answered.

"I thought you would. You guys know all the best people."

"That's why you love us so much," Kate snarked back.

"Are they back there?" Nathan asked, pointing to the glass partition and door on the far side of the hallway.

"In the room of death, yes," he replied. "It'll be right up your street, this one."

"Oh?" Kate asked as they started across the hallway.

"Check out the books and the décor in the library."

Kate nodded and hurried after Nathan, who was already on his way to the back of the entrance hall, where there were several more officers. As they approached the open glass door, Damon walked out of the room that Luis had called a library.

"I thought I heard you," he said and offered his hand.

Nathan shook it. "Damon."

Kate followed suit.

"Good to see you. Thanks for getting here quickly."

"Anytime," Nathan replied.

"What do we have?" Kate asked.

"I can't say for sure, but I think we might have another Black Hand incident. It certainly fits with their MO. Come on, follow me," Damon replied and led them over to the glass door as he spoke. "The victim is Alister Langley. He's the owner of this house, and they killed him in his library. I've been aware of Alister for a while, he's a collector and trader of esoteric and occult books and assorted items. But he's mainly interested in the books, hence the library," he explained as he stepped into the room.

"He's spent some money on this," Kate remarked, noticing the solid glass door with its sleek locking mechanism and security pad.

"He did," Damon confirmed. "The glass door and walls are ballistic glass, and the room is usually controlled for both temperature and humidity to keep the books preserved. He wanted to protect his collection."

"I'm guessing someone wanted something, though?" Kate asked.

"That would be my guess," Damon replied. "But we can't see anything obvious that's been stolen."

As she examined the door and the surrounding area, she spotted a camera mounted up on the ceiling. "Security's good. Do we have the feed?" she asked, pointing up at the camera.

"The tech guys are on it," Damon replied. "Don't worry, you'll have everything."

"Alright, let's see him," Nathan said.

Damon nodded and led them through the shelving to a central open area in the middle of the room. On a table that was meant to be used for study, the body of a man in his fifties lay on his back. His stomach was sliced open, with some of his innards trailing out, over the table and down to the floor as blood pooled around him.

The room stank, but it was a smell that Kate had experienced many times before. She'd never say she was used to it, you never got used to that smell, but it was an expected part of the job.

It was much stronger next to the body, though. One of the SOCOs wandered over to them, clipboard in hand.

"Morning guys," Sheridan greeted them. Only her eyes were visible, the rest of her was covered in a white coverall, complete with hood and mask. "Another day, another body."

"Looks that way. What do you have?" Nathan asked.

"Cause of death is fairly obvious," she answered. "He suffered multiple stab wounds to his body that damaged several of his internal organs, but it's likely he took a while to finally pass. My guess would be they were trying to torture him. I think the time of death was likely not far off about eleven PM. As you can see, there's blood everywhere. We have a couple of fairly obvious leads, such as boot prints. We've lifted a few prints as well, so we'll see who they belong to. That said, I think the best evidence will be the security feed."

"I agree," Nathan answered.

"So, he was a collector?" Kate asked as she looked at some of the tomes on the shelves that surrounded them. There were a few framed images on the walls too, showing off curious pictograms and designs that were not dissimilar to the strange markings she'd seen both Wilson Hollins and Solomon Lichwood use at the sites of their murders.

"He was. We try to keep a close eye on those who deal with the organisations that trade in questionable items such as these. Alister was one of them. He had dealings with several of the world's more secretive and powerful groups who have links to mysticism and the occult. There was a lot of money changing hands, and he got quite rich off the back of it. That made him a person of interest for us. I don't remember much beyond that, as he's a smaller player in a much bigger game, but I can bring his file to the station for you."

"Any family or anything?"

"I don't know," Damon replied. "I'd have to pull his file, but we can find out."

"We can do some digging ourselves, as well," Nathan added.

"Who found him and called it in?" Kate asked.

"The cleaner," Damon replied.

"Dyson?" Nathan asked, giving Kate a wry smile. Kate rolled her eyes and Damon pulled a face. "Sorry, private joke. You were saying?"

Damon blinked as Kate glanced back at Luis Dyson who'd looked their way on hearing his name, but he shrugged and went about his job.

"Her name is Ivona Kijek. She's in one of the other rooms giving her statement and a few other bits."

"Mind if I go and say hi?" Kate asked.

"Go ahead," Damon said.

"I'll come with you," Nathan replied, and followed her out and into another room where a uniformed officer was just finishing up.

"Hi," Kate greeted her, showing Ivona her warrant card. "Mind if we ask you some questions?"

"I just gave my statement," the woman replied in an Eastern European accent, apparently not keen to repeat the information she'd just given. She was perhaps in her late forties, with wild dark hair and a kind face.

"It'll only take a few minutes," Kate reassured her.

Ivona sighed. "Sure, okay."

"Good, thank you," Kate replied and sat down in a seat opposite. "So, tell me what happened. What did you see?"

"I didn't see anything. I left here yesterday, as usual. Alister was normal. He didn't seem worried about anything or upset. I came here today and started work..."

"You have a key?" Kate interrupted.

"Yes. I have a key. I let myself in and got started, but noticed the smell. That's when I found the library door open."

"Is that unusual?"

"Oh yes. He never leaves that door open. I'm not allowed in there, and he only goes in occasionally. But when I saw the door left open, I knew something was wrong. That was when I saw him, through the glass."

"And then you called us?"

"Yes, right away."

"Good," Nathan said.

"So, tell me about Alister. Was he nice?"

"Oh yes. He was very good to me. He pays me very well, but now, I think I don't have a job."

"I'm sure you'll find more work," Nathan replied. "This is Surrey."

Kate nodded She didn't want to offer any false promises and needed to focus on the job at hand. She felt terribly sorry for the woman, to have her income ripped away so suddenly, but there wasn't much they could do, so she continued with her line of questioning. "So, was he planning on something last night? Did he have anyone coming over?"

"I don't know. I try not to pry."

"So he had no one coming to visit him?"

"I don't think so. Well, I don't know. He does sometimes have… Um… You know, ladies, who he pays, come to the house. Sometimes they stay the night, and I see them in the morning."

"You mean escorts?" Kate asked.

"Yes," Ivona replied, pleased that Kate had found the word for her. "He sometimes sees escorts."

Chapter 6

"Okay, if we're ready?" Nathan asked everyone in the Incident Room. Their usual team was all here, with the addition of Damon from the National Crime Agency who would be joining them and helping them out on this case.

"The victim is Alister Langley," Nathan began. "He was fifty-six, a resident of Send, and a collector of rare and valuable books and other items. He was apparently killed in his library, which suggests that maybe the killer was after something. There was nothing obvious missing, but there were hundreds of books in that room, so it could be a while before we know for sure. Sheridan?"

Nathan moved aside as the Scene of Crime officer stood up before the group. No longer concealed beneath her white coveralls, she wore a more typical police uniform and let her blonde hair fall loose over her shoulders.

"Thanks. So we have the time of death at around eleven last night. We believe he died from massive blood loss due to multiple stab wounds that damaged several internal organs, but we'll know more once the coroner has had a chance to go over the body. Meanwhile, we'll be working on prints and seeing if we can match them up to anyone who shouldn't have been at the house."

"Thank you, Sheridan. Damon?"

The short man stood and adjusted his round-rim glasses. "Thank you, Nathan, and thank you all for allowing me to join you. I'll try not to get in your way."

"You won't," DC Rachel Arthur said, and then winked at Kate.

Damon smiled. "Oh, good," he replied happily, and then frowned, wondering if Rachel had been commenting about his height. He glanced at Kate. She nodded to him, knowing full well that his height was the very thing that Rachel was referring to. He was not a tall man and was, in fact, shorter than everyone else in the room.

"Okay, well, we've been aware of Mr Langley for a while. He wasn't someone we were too worried about, nor was he a major player, but I certainly recognised the name. He's a collector of rare books on occult subjects, but he's also a trader, buying and selling items to and from organisations like the Black Hand."

"The group responsible for the Hollins and Solomon cases?" Zafar asked.

"Possibly responsible," Kate clarified. "We don't have any hard evidence yet."

"Okay, yeah, sure. But it's very likely linked to them, right? That's why you're here," he said, pointing at Damon.

"That's right. I've been investigating these organisations on behalf of the NCA for several years now, and it's my belief that the Black Hand was at least linked to the cases you mentioned, if not outright ordered or sponsored by them."

"And you think they're doing the same with his one?" DC Faith Evanson asked.

"I think that's very likely, yes," Damon replied. "Within the market itself, Alister was well known, travelled a lot, and was someone to go to if you wanted certain items found. He was well-connected."

"Do we have anything on Alister on our end?" Nathan asked.

Rachel stood. She wore a suit similar to Kate's and had her hair tied up at the back of her head. "We have a few things. Not much in the way of a family really, the only one I could find was a sister who lives in Shere. Their parents died a while back."

"Anything in regards to work friends? Colleagues and such?" Nathan asked Damon.

"I'll need to look at his file, but I seem to remember we had some associates listed. One other thing we know, which was confirmed by the cleaner who found him, was that he was a frequent user of escort agencies."

"That's right," Kate said. "Ivona confirmed that when we spoke to her. She'd sometimes meet them if they stayed the night."

"Classy," Rachel commented.

"Okay," Nathan said, stepping forward. "We need to know much more about our victim. Who was he? Who did he associate with? Whatever you can find on him. Dion?"

"Sir?" DC Dion Dyer replied.

"We'll hopefully have some security footage come through from the tech guys, so wrangle that and go through it. Faith, we'll be taking a trip over to speak with his sister, if you'd like to join us in your role as Victim Support, that would be great."

"Will do, guv," Faith replied.

"Do we have a name for the sister?" Kate asked.

Rachel checked her notes. "Alison Chambers. A married name, I guess."

"Thanks. Print out a copy of whatever you have so we can take it with us, will you? We'll be grabbing a quick bite to eat before we set off. Grab your things, Faith, we'll leave in ten, fifteen tops."

Faith nodded.

"Alright, dismissed. Now, where's my sandwich?"

Kate got up, left the Incident Room, and made for her desk. She dropped into her seat and ripped open the cardboard packaging of her cheese and pickle sandwich. Her stomach rumbled as the smell reached her nose, making her mouth water, before she finally took a bite and savoured the taste.

They'd spent much of their morning at the crime scene, before returning to the station. They'd picked up something to eat on the way, but hadn't had a chance to eat it until now. She looked up to see Nathan tucking into his food as he checked his email.

As Kate munched her way through her sandwich, she scrolled through the messages on her phone and noticed an email address she didn't recognise. But it wasn't so much the sender's address that caught her attention, it was the subject line.

It was one word.

Jethro.

The name of Francine's butchered cat.

Her first thought was that one of her flatmates had heard of the cat's demise and was emailing her about it. Curious, she opened it, but the body of the email was blank. The only thing the email contained was an attachment. The filename was a string of random letters, but it ended in .jpg.

Curious, she tapped on the file and the image opened up.

Kate stopped chewing her food as she stared at the image on her phone's screen.

It was a photo of Jethro, clearly alive, and clearly distressed. A fist held a knife embedded in the cat's belly as blood welled up around it.

Kate tapped the 'back' symbol on her phone as a wave of nausea washed over her. She swallowed her food and placed the rest down on her desk, along with her phone. Kate sat back in her chair and took a deep breath, as the image she'd just seen burned bright in her mind's eye.

"Shit," she quietly cursed to herself. It was him. She was sure of it. He had her email address and was taunting her. He was showing her what he'd done. She felt helpless. She didn't know what to do. No one, apart from her and her aunt's killer, knew what she'd done all those years ago, and there was no way she was ever going to tell anyone else.

Not voluntarily, anyway.

But then, maybe she'd have that choice taken away from her. Maybe this psycho would force her hand and she'd have to tell someone.

But who?

Nathan was the obvious choice. He'd be the one most likely to take her side and see things from her perspective. But what if he didn't? What if he told the DCI? Or the Chief? What then? But even if he did take her side, what could he do? He was little better than a character witness.

But that wasn't what Fiona's killer wanted, she mused. He wanted to hold it over her head and use it as a weapon to get what he wanted. Whatever that was. Maybe it wasn't anything specific. Maybe just having a police officer in his pocket was benefit enough.

If he did use it though, he'd want to ruin her. Destroy her career and turn her into a laughing stock, or worse still, a criminal, like him.

She sighed, picked up her phone, and deleted the email.

She'd cross that bridge when she came to it. She didn't see the need to tell anyone what she'd done, at least not yet.

Popping her phone back on her desk, Kate woke her PC up and logged in. She opened up her police email account and scanned through the emails, checking several of them out. There was nothing much of interest until she opened one up from the Case for the Prosecution against Wilson Hollins.

She raised an eyebrow. Why were they emailing her? She scanned through the body of the email and her stomach sank. The team had been continuing to work on some of Hollins' hard drives from the computer they'd confiscated from the commercial unit where they'd arrested him. They had just recently cracked the security on one of them. Inside, they'd found, amongst other things, records of emails that Hollins had sent to an unknown email address they were having trouble tracing. The emails had all contained videos, which had all been taken from the cameras in her apartment. Which was why they were emailing her.

Wilson had been emailing personal videos of her to someone.

Kate looked at the email again, and suddenly realised she recognised it. Grabbing her phone, she opened up her email client and clicked into the deleted items.

She swallowed. The address Hollins had been sending the videos to was the same one that Fiona's killer had just emailed her the cat photo from.

Chapter 7

Kate watched the stone houses approach as Nathan drove into the idyllic, quintessentially English village of Shere, deep in the Surrey countryside. Her mind was a million miles away from the chocolate box scenery that surrounded her and instead, was in much darker places filled with mutilated cats and murdered people.

She thought about the photo she'd been sent. She thought about Hollins sending Fiona's killer videos of her doing God only knew what in the privacy of her own home, and she thought about the butchered cat.

As these thoughts passed through her mind, she couldn't help but think of the clear link they had to the way Alister Langley had been killed.

Was the man who killed Alister the same one that killed Fiona?

Was that man up to his old tricks again?

If he was, what would happen next? She was supposed to be investigating this murder. Was he planning to blackmail her into messing up the investigation? Or was she reading far too much into this?

There was a link there, between her aunt's killer and Alister's death. There had to be. It was too much of a coincidence that all this should happen on the same day.

"You know they shot some of Bridget Jones's Diary here, right?" Faith said from the back seat of the car.

"What?" Kate asked.

"Bridget Jones's Diary," Faith repeated. "They shot some of that movie here, in Shere."

"I think everyone in Surrey knows that," Nathan replied.

"Did they? I didn't know that," Kate answered, glad to be distracted from her murky thoughts.

"Yep. It was the church scene, wasn't it?" Faith asked.

"I dunno," Nathan answered. "I don't watch chick flicks like that."

"More of an action-adventure guy, are we?" Kate asked.

Nathan gave her side-eye but didn't answer.

"The Holiday, they shot some of that here, too," Faith said.

"The one with Jude Law in it?" Kate asked.

"That's the one."

"Oh, cool. I'll have to watch them again, see if I recognise anything."

"It's all messed up, though. They go to the village pub, but that was filmed somewhere else entirely. I mean, I suppose the Yanks won't notice, but it was a bit jarring to me."

Kate smiled. "The Yanks?"

"What? That's not a bad word, is it?"

"I have no idea," Kate admitted. "Just sounded funny the way you said it."

"Well, I'm glad I amuse you," Faith replied. "So, are we nearly there?"

"Nearly," Nathan answered. "Remind me of their names again?"

"Alison and Jerry Chambers," Faith said.

Kate put on a fake laugh that stopped abruptly and looked back at Faith who wore a strange expression. "What? You amuse me."

Faith rolled her eyes.

Kate laughed.

Over the next few minutes, they guided Nathan to the house that was a stone's throw from the centre of the village, before pulling up on the narrow street.

The house was a modest affair and had clearly been there for decades at least.

"Lead the way," Nathan said, stepping aside. He often let her do the talking during interviews, as he believed she was better with people than he was.

Kate knocked on the front door and waited. Moments later it was opened by a middle-aged woman who looked at them curiously. "Um, hello?"

"Mrs Chambers?" Kate asked.

"Yes?" the woman replied.

Kate held up her warrant card. "I'm Detective O'Connell, this is Detective Halliwell and Detective Evanson." They held up their ID as well. "Could we come inside and talk?"

"Um, yes. Of course. What is this about?"

"It's better if we talk inside," Kate replied.

"Oh, well, if you say so."

"Is your husband home?"

She nodded. "Jerry? Come here."

"What's up?" a voice shouted from the back of the house.

"It's the police," she called back.

There was silence for a moment. A few seconds later, a man walked into the hall wearing a frown. "Did you say 'the police'?"

"I'm Detective O'Connell," Kate repeated. "Nice to meet you, sir."

"Oh, hi," he said and offered his hand. Kate shook it.

"Can we speak somewhere more comfortable?" Kate asked.

"Of course, come through."

They moved into the lounge where Kate sat beside Nathan on the sofa. Faith stood to one side as the Chambers both sat down.

"I'm afraid I have some bad news," Kate began.

"Oh?" Mrs Chambers asked.

"Your brother, Alister Langley, was murdered last night. I'm so sorry."

"Oh god," Alison gasped, clamping a hand over her mouth as her eyes welled up.

"Murdered?" Jerry asked.

"Yes. There was a break-in at his property and he was killed during the incident. We're just beginning our investigation."

Alison nodded. "What… Why…? I don't…" She seemed to sigh as she thought things through. "I told him to be careful. Did they steal anything from that library of his?"

"We don't know," Kate admitted. "We're looking into it. But, what do you mean, 'you told him to be careful'?"

Alison choked back some more tears and sniffed. "Sorry."

"It's okay. Take your time. Faith here is what we call a Victim Support Officer. We'll leave her here with you for a little while, so you can talk, and she'll visit regularly, but we just need to ask you a few questions."

Alison nodded.

"It was only a matter of time," Jerry said. He didn't seem very upset over the news.

"What do you mean?" Kate asked.

Jerry shook his head. "He was into some weird shit. Books on magic and stuff. But not like, stage tricks, you know?

Books on what he called 'real magic'. Witchcraft and crap like that. It's all bollocks, of course, but he loved it."

"And that was dangerous?" Kate pressed.

"He mixed with strange people," Alison answered. "I didn't know much about what he did. He kept that part to himself and wouldn't talk to me about it much. Didn't want me getting involved, he'd say. Too dangerous. I wasn't sure what to make of it, but when I went round there once, one of his clients was just leaving. He was a really creepy guy."

"Oh?"

"Yeah. Alister wasn't pleased that I'd shown up early. Told me never to do that again."

"Interesting. Would you be willing to look at some mugshots later to see if you recognise anyone?"

"Yes, of course," Alison replied.

Kate nodded her thanks. "Tell me more about your relationship with Alister. Were you close?"

"Not really," Jerry said.

"Yes and no," Alison replied. "We were, and we weren't. We'd speak almost every day. He was always really interested in what I was up to. He'd listen quite happily to whatever boring stuff I'd done that day. He didn't ever really talk to me about his work. Although, we both kind of knew what it was he did." She looked over at Jerry as she spoke.

"Yeah, we knew."

"But he would never talk about it," Alison continued. "He'd talk about other stuff…"

"Ugh, yeah," Jerry said.

"Like what?" Kate pressed.

"Look, he was a nice man, really. His work was a little…odd. But he was alright. It's just that, he would sometimes…"

She seemed to be having difficulty verbalising what she was trying to tell them. Kate wanted to make a suggestion based on what she already knew, but she also didn't want to lead the witness.

"He's a dirty old man," Jerry cut across her.

"He wasn't," Alison protested.

"Oh, come on. You know as well as I do what he did. He'd hire escorts, young women. To have sex with them, you know?"

"Not personally, but yes, I'm aware," Kate replied.

"He was lonely," Alison said.

"We're not judging him, Mrs Chambers," Kate reassured her. "We just need to know as much about him as we can. You never know what might help us find his killer."

Alison nodded. "He calls me most days. Well, called, I guess. He'd listen to what I'd been up to, and then he always told me about his day, but never about his work. So, he'd tell me what he ate for lunch and stuff, what TV he'd been watching, that kind of thing. He was always very open about the girls he hired, too. Went into quite a lot of detail about them. Not what he does with them, but he's always telling...told... me who they are and what they were like."

"Did he call you yesterday? Did he tell you what his plans were last night?"

"Oh yes. He called. Told me he'd hired a girl called Rosa for last night. One of his regulars, apparently. Honestly, I don't take too much interest in all that, it's just not what I want to hear, you know?"

"It's disgusting," Jerry cut in. "A fifty-year-old man sleeping with these twenty-somethings? It's wrong if you ask me."

"He was happy," Alison protested.

"I bet," Jerry replied. Kate sensed a hint of jealousy in the comment and wondered if he wasn't actually disgusted but instead, was jealous that Alister was sleeping with all of those young women, when Jerry couldn't because he was married.

"So was there anything else? Was he worried about anything? Was he having any trouble? Maybe he was in debt to someone? Anything that might hint at someone wanting to hurt him?" Kate asked.

"No, nothing like that. Nothing that hadn't been an issue for decades anyway."

"So, nothing unusual?"

Alison shook her head. "Sorry."

"That's okay. But if you think of anything, please get in touch with us, alright?"

"Of course."

Kate and Nathan left the house, leaving Faith to stay with the couple for now. Someone would come and pick her up later.

"We need to find Rosa," Nathan said as they returned to the car.

"I'd bet my life on that being a fake name," Kate said.

"Oh, that's a given. They never use their real names."

Kate climbed in and sat beside Nathan. "You know that for certain, do you?" Meaning lacing her words.

Nathan smiled. All learnt in the line of duty."

"I bet."

"We should look at what escort agencies are local to Send and see if we get a hit on Rosa."

"You want to hit on Rosa?"

"Oh, you're on fire today, Kate."

She smiled, licked her finger, and pressed it to her thigh, making a hissing sound as she did so.

Nathan rolled his eyes as Kate felt her phone buzz.

"Go," she said as she held it to her ear.

"We just got word from a Guildford detective," Rachel said on the other end of the line. "There's an escort at

Guildford Hospital who says she'd been booked by Alister Langley, but she was stopped on her way to his house and beaten up before being left on the side of the road."

"Let me guess," Kate replied. "Her name is Rosa."

"How did you know that?"

Chapter 8

"We're looking for a Detective Burns?" Nathan asked the nurse on the reception desk.

She pointed up the hallway, and Kate looked up to see a man sat outside a ward. Everything about him screamed detective.

"Thanks," Kate said and walked up the hall with Nathan.

"Detective Burns?" Nathan asked.

The man, who looked to be in this thirties, looked up. "Detectives Halliwell and O'Connell?"

"I'm Halliwell, this is O'Connell," Nathan clarified, flashing his warrant card.

"Hey," Kate greeted him.

"Hi. So, you're on the Langley Case, then?"

"That's right, and I think you found our missing escort," Nathan replied.

"Looks that way."

"So, what happened?" Kate asked.

"We got a call from a concerned woman who'd found Rosa naked in the street. She'd been badly beaten. Covered in cuts and bruises. She had some broken ribs, too. Whoever did this really made a mess of her.

"Is she conscious?"

"She is. She gave us a statement, that's when the link to your case came up. Do you want to speak to her?"

"Please," Nathan replied.

"This way," the Detective said, leading them into the ward.

The room was lined on either side by three beds, and all six of them were occupied. Their victim was in the end bed on the right, with the curtains drawn. Burns walked around the blue curtain.

"Rosa? I have some people here to speak with you."

"Okay..." a weak voice replied.

Kate stepped beyond the curtain and got her first good look at Rosa. Burns wasn't kidding, they'd really worked her over. Her face was swollen in several places, with sticky sutures holding a couple of cuts closed. She could barely see out of one eye.

"Hi," Kate said quietly.

"Thank you for seeing us," Nathan added.

"That's okay. Do you want to know what happened, too?"

Kate nodded. "We believe your assault is closely linked to a case we're leading, so you'll be dealing with us from now on."

"Oh? What case?"

Kate looked at Nathan, who nodded once, clearly understanding what Kate was wondering. "You were going to Mr Langley's residence last night, right?"

Rosa sighed. "Yeah, that's right. He's one of my regulars. Nice guy."

"Well, I'm sorry to be the one to tell you this, but he was murdered last night."

"Oh," Rosa answered, and took a breath. She took a moment, looking into her lap before she looked up. "I did wonder…"

"We think he might have been killed by the same people who attacked you."

"Makes sense."

"Can you tell us what happened last night?" Nathan pressed.

"I was forced off the road by a couple of cars," she said with a haunted look in her eyes. "I didn't know what to do. I couldn't get away. There were four of them. Three guys and a girl. They dragged me from my car and just started hitting me and kicking me. I thought I was going to die."

"I cannot imagine how that must have felt," Kate sympathised. "But you're okay now. You're safe."

Rosa nodded.

"We need to find them. We need to catch them so no one else suffers, and we need your help to do it."

"Of course. Anything I can do to help."

Kate gave her a small nod and a smile. "Did they speak to you. Did you hear any names? Anything about their appearance that might help us identify them?"

"I... I don't know. There were three guys. The one who I think was leading them, he was bald. They were all big guys. Strong, you know?"

"We understand," Nathan replied.

"You said there was a woman?"

"Yeah. She helped. She was smaller than the others, with dark hair. But she was just as into it. She helped them strip me. They took my clothes."

"If we brought in a sketch artist, could you work with them to try and work out what they looked like?"

"Um, yeah, I guess," Rosa replied.

"I take it Rosa isn't your real name?" Nathan asked.

"No. Sorry. It's Ruta. Ruta Marek."

"And can you tell us the name of the agency you work for?" Kate asked.

Ruta nodded. "Viva Escorts, in Guildford," she answered in hushed tones.

"Thank you, Ruta,"

"I hope you find them," she said.

Kate nodded. "We will. Do you happen to have an address for the agency?"

Chapter 9

As they drove into Guildford, the sun dipped lower on the horizon and evening drew in around them.

"What did you make of her?" Kate asked.

"She seemed willing to help, and if we can get into Alister's hard drives and pull the security feed, she might be able to confirm if it's the same people who attacked her."

"It sounds like there was a whole crew involved," Kate replied. "The woman she mentioned must have played the part of the escort."

"That would be my assumption too," Nathan answered. "She gains entry, distracts Alister while her friends break-in, and then they attack him."

Kate frowned. "But why not just break-in? Why go to the trouble of pretending to be an escort?"

"The library," Nathan suggested. "She persuaded Alister to open up the library so they could get whatever it was they wanted."

"Which means there must be something missing, then. A book or something."

"That would make sense," Nathan agreed.

"We still don't know the whole picture, though," Kate mused. "What item were they stealing, and why?"

"Yep," Nathan answered. "We don't know the motive behind it either, or how it relates to the Black Hand."

"Or even if it does relate to the Black Hand. It might not."

Nathan nodded.

"Damon thinks it does though, but is he chasing shadows?"

"All we can do is keep digging," Nathan replied as they pulled onto a street just a short distance from the centre of town.

There were a few shops along one end of the road, and when Kate checked the address that Ruta had given her, she quickly picked out a single door between two shop windows.

"There," Kate said.

"I see it," Nathan replied and parked up. They crossed the road and Kate scanned the labels beside the intercom just to the side of the door. Only two were used. One of them was a name she didn't recognise and the other just said Viva.

Kate pressed the button. The intercom buzzed quietly. Seconds passed, and then the speaker crackled into life.

"Hello?"

"Hi," Kate replied. "We'd like to speak with a Marcy Westcott, please?"

"Who's calling?"

"My name's Detective O'Connell, we just need a few moments of your time."

"Right," the voice replied, and the intercom clicked off.

Kate looked at the metal box and then at the door, before glancing back at Nathan with a questioning look.

"Police aren't usually very friendly with sex workers, so…"

Kate frowned and pressed the button again.

"What?" the voice asked.

"We just need to speak with—."

"Piss off." The connection clicked off again.

Kate grunted and stabbed the button.

The voice crackled into life for the third time. "Look, I told you—,"

Kate was in no mood to be messing about and interrupted. "One of your workers was beaten up, impersonated by someone who then killed one of your clients last night. We need to talk to you."

The connection crackled but didn't close. The person on the other end didn't say anything for several moments.

"Fine." The connection closed again, and then the door unlocked.

Kate pushed it open and looked back at Nathan with a smug grin.

"Impressive."

"Thanks."

They were stood in a thin stairwell that led up to the first floor. It was poorly lit and there was a cloying smell that Kate wrinkled her nose at. At the top of the stairs a door opened and a woman in her late forties leaned out as cigarette smoke wafted around her.

"Come up," she urged, sounding annoyed at the intrusion before taking a pull on her cigarette.

Kate nodded and led the way up the well-worn linoleum stairs with metal edging. At the top, the woman stepped back into the apartment and held the door open for them. Red curtains were drawn over the windows, dropping the room into shadow that was hardly relieved by the red bulb in the main light. The woman gestured to a table near the door and sat down opposite them.

"What's this about?" she asked with a sigh.

"Are you Marcy Westcott?"

"So what if I am?"

"We've been told that you run the Viva Escort Agency. Is that correct?"

"I don't know. That's difficult to answer."

"No, it isn't," Kate replied, annoyed with the woman's attitude. "Look, I don't give a shit what you do for a living right now, okay? That's not why we're here. We're here because a man is dead, and one of your girls, who was booked to see him last night was beaten to within an inch of her life and left for dead on the side of the road. *They* are my priority right now. But if you want to make life difficult for us, and impede our investigation, then I'll make sure to slap every charge against you that I can. Or you can talk, show some compassion towards the girls you employ, and then get on with your evening."

She didn't quite know where that little outburst came from. What Kate did know was that this woman's attitude and apparent disregard for her escorts had rubbed her the wrong way. She was moments away from arresting her and dragging her down to the station.

The woman looked more than a little shocked by the dressing down, too. Maybe she'd underestimated Kate. Maybe she'd thought that this young police detective wasn't that tough. Well, Kate was more than happy to show her just how much grit she had, if it came to that.

The woman sat back and took a long drag on her cigarette, before pressing it into the ashtray on the table. She blew the smoke above her and then returned her gaze to Kate.

"I'm Marcy," she replied. "What happened? Is this about Rosa?"

"Then you know something happened."

"I knew she didn't come back when she said she would, and hasn't been answering my calls. Thought she'd done a runner."

Kate leant forward, placing her arms on the table. "Rosa, or Ruta, is in hospital, Marcy. She was forced off the road by a gang who knew where she was going. She was beaten, stripped, and robbed before they left her there to die. Luckily, she's a tough one. She managed to move, and someone found her."

"Fuck," Marcy replied.

"Indeed. So we need to know what you know about Rosa's job last night and the man she was going to see. Alister Langley."

Marcy nodded. "He's a regular... or was, I guess. Called up every week to book one of the girls. They got to know him, he got to know them. He paid well and was always respectful. The girls liked going to him."

"Well, unfortunately, one of the gang members took Rosa's place. They got into Alister's house and killed him."

"Shit. So, he's dead now."

"Mmm-hmm."

"Damn it. He was a good one."

"Well, I'm sorry for your loss."

Marcy shrugged. She didn't seem terribly upset.

"Can you tell us anything else? Has anyone been sniffing around lately? Have any of the girls reported being followed? Has anything happened to suggest that someone has been watching you in the last few weeks?"

Marcy shook her head. "Nothing unusual like that, no. This is all news to me."

"What about your girls? Can you ask them?"

"I can ask, sure. Doubt there'll be anything, though. They always tell me if someone's being an ass."

"So, how would someone know when one of your girls was heading to Alister's?"

"I dunno. Maybe they just watched. He was always regular as clockwork. Same time, same day, every week. It's an easy pattern to learn."

Kate nodded and glanced over at Nathan who'd been taking notes. He looked up and nodded back to her.

"Alright, I think that's it for now. But don't skip town, alright?"

"Wouldn't dream of it," Marcy replied as she pulled another cigarette from the pack on the table.

"Thank you, Mrs Westcott."

"Yeah, yeah," she muttered. "Show yourselves out."

"Well, she was helpful," Kate said sarcastically as they crossed the road to their car.

"She's only looking out for herself and her girls. Doesn't want to get shut down."

Kate nodded as she reached the car and looked back at the curtained windows of the upper floor apartment.

"Yeah, I know."

"I think I saw another side of you in there."

"Didn't think I had it in me?"

"You certainly showed her who's boss."

"I was just fed up with her crap."

"So, what do you think?"

"I think she's right," Kate admitted. "It would be easy to work out the pattern since he ordered a girl every week like clockwork. Then you work out the best place to ambush them and boom, you're in business."

"That was my assessment, too."

Chapter 10

Kate woke up with a start, sitting bolt upright in bed.

Beside her, her phone finished buzzing as its green LED flashed, alerting her to a new message.

She sighed and picked up her phone. Its screen flared to life, nearly blinding her. She took a moment to let her eyes adjust to the light, wiping away the tears that had welled up. Moments later she could finally read the message. It was from Rachel.

'Come in. We've got the security video.'

Kate quickly tapped a reply.

'Be right there,' and plopped her phone back on her nightstand.

She stretched and yawned. Gave herself a scratch, and then suddenly noticed the fresh envelope on the floor by the door.

"Aaah, crap." She swung her legs out of bed and eyed the letter, getting that sinking feeling in her stomach again as she wondered what might be inside.

Standing up, she crossed the room and picked it up. She noted the now-familiar writing on the front that spelt out her name, before ripping it open.

Inside was a single sheet of folded up paper. She unfolded it to find that there were photos of all her flatmates on there. Francine, Clyde, Aziz, Jaida, and the others, all were smiling to the camera. The images had probably come from somewhere online. Aziz didn't have that hairstyle anymore.

At the top, a simple phrase asked, 'Who do I kill first?' Beneath each photo was a checkbox, waiting for her to fill it in.

Disgusted, she tore the paper to shreds and flung the remains into her bin.

Was that his play, then? Was that what he was going to do to make things a little more favourable for him? Threaten the people she knew? Would he then try to blackmail her?

She paced across her room as she turned all the possibilities over in her mind. Should she tell Nathan? Should she warn her flatmates? Should she just ignore it all and hope for the best?

Returning to her bed she flopped onto her side, buried her head in her pillow and screamed.

***

Kate wandered into the incident room, clutching a cardboard cup of coffee she'd picked up from a service station on her way over. It was still piping hot.

Nathan, Dion, Rachel, and Debby were all present, sitting and talking.

"Morning," Kate said as she walked in. "I see the press got hold of it. It was on the radio on the way in."

"DCI Dean handled that," Nathan said.

Kate nodded. "Fair enough.

"Did we wake you?" Rachel asked.

"What do you think?" Kate replied, allowing a strong note of sarcasm to tinge her words.

"Sorry," Rachel replied.

"It's okay, I wanted to know as soon as we had the footage."

"Well, we got it, alright."

"Is it good?"

"Sure is," Rachel replied. "It's blockbuster material."

"Have you seen it?" Kate asked Nathan.

"No, I just got here moments before you. Do we see the murder?" Nathan asked.

"We can see everything," Rachel answered. "Alister was really hot on his security."

"And not just with the number of cameras in his place," Dion added. "The security videos were locked up tight in an encrypted file. I would never have gotten in, but we contacted the company that runs the online storage he used, and they granted us access."

"That took a while," Kate replied, surprised.

"They're not in the UK," Rachel replied. "We had to convince them of who we were."

"There's still loads more to go through," Dion continued, "and most of that is still encrypted."

"I see. Well, at least we got the video. Let's see them."

"They're a bit gory," Dion warned her.

"Don't worry, I have my big girl pants on."

"Nathan told us about your run-in with the madam," Rachel said.

"Oh, did he?" Kate glanced over at Nathan.

Nathan blinked at her. "What?"

"Nothing. Yeah, I had to have a little chat with her. Let her know which side her bread was buttered."

"Nice," Dion replied.

Kate raised an eyebrow at him. "You like that, do you?"

"Nothing quite like a strong woman kicking ass and taking names," he replied.

"Is that right?" I'll keep that in mind," Kate commented.

"You're in there," Rachel goaded him, elbowing him in the arm.

"Ow, that hurt."

"Wimp," Rachel snarked. "Sounds like you need a strong woman to look after your ass."

"You offering? I have a nice ass," he quipped back.

"Eww, gross," Kate commented.

"She started it," Dion deflected.

"Where are all the strong men when you need them, huh?" Rachel said. "Play the video, Conan the Barbarian."

"Right you are, Wonder Woman."

"See, you're getting it," Rachel replied to him as he opened a video file and clicked play.

"So, what am I looking at here?" Kate asked. It took her a moment to orient herself, but then she suddenly understood she was looking at the entrance lobby of Alister Langley's house. Two seconds later, he walked into the frame and opened the front door. A woman in a tiny dress stood on the other side, her hip kicked out, looking very much like a confident escort.

"Now, watch this, this is interesting," Dion said. He clicked a button, and the video shrunk back to one of several feeds from multiple cameras. As she watched, Alister and the girl talked at the door for a few moments, and then he let her in before moving to a keypad by the door and doing something.

A second later, the handful of feeds that were being recorded suddenly tripled.

"What did he do?" Kate asked.

"I think our victim was a little suspicious of the fake hooker," Nathan replied.

"Of course," Kate replied. "He knew he'd booked Rosa, but it wasn't Rosa who turned up."

"So he turned on the extra cameras, just in case," Nathan finished.

"Clever boy," Kate added, watching as Alister and the escort talked and occasionally got intimate before he finally opened the door to the library.

"Look here," Dion said, pointing to another feed. Kate looked over, and as the door to the library opened, which made some noise with the locks and the hissing of the air, the house's back door was forced open.

"They knew what they were doing," Kate said. "That was well-timed."

"He never heard them," Nathan agreed.

As Alister and the escort moved into the library, and onto some HD feed, Kate watched the team of four men, led by a large, bald man, walk through the house. They walked up behind Alister and the lead man hit him on the back of the head with the butt of his gun.

Alister dropped to the floor.

The library's cameras recorded sound, and she could hear their voices. She watched Alister defy the man, and then the man pulled his shirt off, revealing his dragon tattoos, before he finally stabbed Alister, announcing himself as the Dragon.

"Shit," Nathan cursed behind her.

Kate turned. "What?"

"I recognise him," Nathan answered.

"You do?"

"Yeah, I do. I'll tell you once we've watched the whole thing."

"Alright. How much more is left?" she asked Dion.

"Just under an hour. We've already watched it. There's not much else to learn. What's clear is that this Dragon dude wants a book. This Liber Exterious, but Alister says he doesn't have it. The Dragon keeps asking, but Alister doesn't move an inch from his story, until eventually, he dies, giving nothing up."

"That takes balls," Rachel commented.

"You'd know," Dion snarked with a grin.

Rachel flipped him the finger.

"The Liber Exterious. What is that, Latin?"

"That's right," Nathan said, stroking his chin, troubled. "Let's watch the rest."

They sat in silence, taking notes as the video played out and they watched Alister die a long and painful death. It wasn't easy to watch and it made Kate feel sick.

"Look," Dion said and played the very end of the video, where the Dragon rummaged around inside Alister's pocket and removed his phone. Then the entire crew left, including the woman who'd pretended to be the escort. She'd joined the Dragon in his torture of Alister by kicking him several times.

"Okay. So they got his phone." Kate turned to Nathan. "Right then, spill it."

The door to the Incident Room opened and Damon walked in. "Did I miss anything?"

"Nothing you can't catch up on," Rachel replied.

"We just watched security footage of the attack," Kate added, "and Nathan recognised the leader of the gang."

"Oh, you do?"

"I recognise the name more than him, but yeah, I'm sure it's the same man."

"Go on, then, tell us," Kate pressed.

"It was a few years back, but it was the case that got me promoted up to lead the Murder Team. The Sandford Case."

"Sandford?" Kate asked.

"Sandford Barret. He was a wealthy, well-connected businessman who killed his mistress. We found her strangled and started the investigation. Everything began to point to Sandford, but then, as we got closer, some of the people we'd spoken to changed their story. They didn't want to talk to us anymore, and the case was going south.

"So, I doubled down and finally got enough to pin it on him. That night, when I was back at home with my then-wife, a gang of men broke in and attacked me."

"Oh, crap," Kate muttered.

"I was certain I was going to die. They had me, and there was nothing we could do. I don't remember much of that night. Not really. But I do remember a bald man who took great pleasure in hurting me, taking off his shirt to show off his dragon tattoo."

"So, what happened?"

"I don't know. They just stopped and left me there as far as I know. I really don't remember too much."

"And the case?" Kate asked.

"Suddenly, several of the key witnesses changed their stories. It was a huge case at the time, and led directly to me getting promoted and leading this team."

"And Sandford?"

"Prison," Nathan replied.

"Then we might need to talk to him."

"I agree," Nathan said. "Dion, get a good shot of all the gang members and print them off."

"On it," Dion replied, and went to work.

"I also have some news," Damon said.

"It never rains, but it pours," Kate replied with a smile. "What do you have?"

"Alister's associates," he answered, and slapped a file down on the table. "There are three main people that I think we should focus on. The one who worked closest with him is

Claire Bissette. She was his research associate and helped him all the time. Then there's Richard Dennell, or Rick as he prefers to be known. He acted as his agent, dealing with Alister's clients and pulling in new business."

"And the third?" Kate asked.

"Bradley Close," Damon replied. "He was Alister's fence. He organised the buying and selling of various artifacts on the black market."

"Do we have addresses for them?"

"I have some for all of them, but they were gathered a while back, so I've no idea what's up to date."

"Alright, so we'll need to look into that."

"I'll leave that with you then," Damon said, sliding the file over to them. "Right, I want to have a look at this video."

Damon joined Dion as Nathan turned back to Kate. "What do you think? What do we do first?"

"I'm not sure. So, this Sandford guy. Do you think he's related to this case?"

"I very much doubt it," Nathan answered. Whoever the Dragon is, he was somehow one of the thugs that got paid to beat me up. I think that might be the limit of the link, but I can't be certain."

"And Sandford, do you think he'll talk?"

"He hates me, so I doubt he'll be very cooperative."

"Alright," Kate answered, trying to get an overview in her mind of the new information they had. "So it's clear that the gang who killed Alister was after a book. A book that was not at Alister's house."

"Yep," Nathan agreed.

"They took his phone, so they possibly have some details about Alister's associates, which puts them in danger."

Nathan nodded. "If they want that book, they're going to go hunting for it."

"Then, I think that's our answer. Sandford isn't going anywhere. I want to talk to him, but he can wait. I think finding and speaking to Alister's associates is more important. We need the book that the gang is looking for."

"Agreed."

"Let's find them, then."

Chapter 11

Nathan pulled the car up on the side road, just a short distance from the village high street in Ripley.

"That's the one," Kate said, nodding to a semi-detached house two doors up from where they'd parked. It was an unremarkable house with a small front garden in a quiet residential street. There was nothing to suggest the person within was some kind of occult researcher who'd been working with Alister Langley.

Kate's phone buzzed.

She popped her finger on the reader at the back, and it woke up, displaying an alert from Rachel.

"Rachel and Zafar are on their way to meet Richard," Kate announced.

"Okay, great. Let's go see what Claire has to say for herself."

Kate nodded, and they left the car behind. Kate took the lead and pressed the doorbell, which rang loudly.

Several seconds later, someone approached from the inside and pressed their face up against the peephole.

Kate smiled at them.

The figure stepped back, fumbled with the chain, and then undid the locks before opening the door. The security chain prevented it from opening very far. A bespectacled face appeared in the gap, her eyes flicking between them.

"Yes?"

Kate held up her ID, detecting a slight French accent in the woman's voice. "Good morning. I'm Detective Kate O'Connell, this is Detective Halliwell. Are you Claire Bissette?"

"Ahh Oui, um, yes. I am. How can I help you, officers?"

"We'd like to speak to you please. Inside, if that's okay?"

The young woman blinked, and then peered past them, looking back and forth, trying to see if anyone else was about. Her gaze returned to Kate and looked her up and down.

"Everything okay?" Kate asked, feeling like she was being examined.

"Hmm? Oh, yes. Hold on." The woman closed the door, released the chain and opened it again, pulling it wide and standing behind it as if she were using it as a shield. "Come in, come in."

Kate nodded, and stepped inside, glancing back at Nathan whose face didn't betray any emotion.

The girl took one last look outside, then shut the door behind them and locked it up again, replacing the chain. She turned and looked at them with a smile. "Can't be too careful, can we?"

"I guess not," Kate replied.

"Come. Come in. Please, sit down. I don't often have visitors."

"Thank you, Miss Bissette. Um, I'm afraid we have some bad news."

"Hmm. This is about Alister, correct? I saw it on the news."

"You know he was murdered, then?"

She sighed. "I do. It's very sad."

"Are you okay? Can you talk?"

"Yes, of course. Cup of tea? Biscuits?"

"Yes, please," Nathan replied.

"Of course, one moment," Claire replied and left the room.

Kate gave Nathan a look. Nathan smirked back, as Kate smiled and looked around the room. Everything about Miss Bissette reminded her of an old woman, but she was certainly no older than thirty. The way she spoke and acted, even the way she decorated her house. She also seemed more than a little paranoid for a twenty-something.

Nathan stepped up beside Kate as she looked over some photos on one of the dressers. "If she brings out Fig Rolls, then that seals it. She's the killer."

Kate snorted. "You think she dresses as a huge bald man on the weekends?"

"You know as well as I do that Fig Rolls are the work of the devil. I wouldn't put anything past those who like them."

"That makes me a…" Kate trailed off as an image of Duane in the wheelchair flashed in her mind.

"Hmmm, maybe I should keep a closer eye on you, then," Nathan quipped

"Maybe you should," she answered, focusing on the photos.

"On the other hand, if she brings out Hobnobs, especially the chocolate ones…then she's an angel from heaven."

"Is all your police work based on biscuits?"

"Isn't yours?" Nathan asked in mock horror.

"I give it less credence than deduction, I'll admit."

"Oh, you heathen," Nathan replied, recoiling slightly.

"Here we go," Claire said as she returned with a tray. On a plate in the middle of the cups, was a pile of Bourbons and Custard Cremes, mixed with Rich Tea biscuits. Kate sat, and smiled over at Nathan, wondering what he'd make of the snacks on offer.

Nathan smiled serenely, plucked a Rich Tea from the plate, and sat back with his tea. Without saying a word, he dunked the biscuit in his drink and bit it.

Claire sat on a chair and picked up her cup, holding it close. "You want to know about him, then? Is that right?"

"Yes," Kate replied. "But first, where were you two nights ago, on the night of the murder?"

"Here," Claire answered. "I spoke with some family and friends on the phone, but I was otherwise alone."

Kate nodded, making a note to check her phone records for the times of the calls, and to check which masts the phone was pinging off. "We'd also like to know about your relationship with Alister. We know what his line of business was, and that you worked as his research assistant, correct?"

"That's right," Claire replied. "He took me on a few years back to help him with cataloguing his books and doing research on some of his finds and on some of the items he was trading. It was good work."

"So, you saw him often, then?"

"Reasonably. I often brought work home with me and studied it here."

"So, he didn't mind lending books out?"

"Not to those he trusted," Claire confirmed.

"Interesting. But there were people he didn't trust, I'm guessing?"

Claire sighed. "I warned him. I told him so many times to be careful. I didn't agree with keeping the more valuable items in his library, but he was convinced it was the safest place."

"It possibly was," Kate said. "But someone didn't mind killing him to get what they wanted."

"Is that the motive, then? They wanted something he had?"

Kate nodded. "We have security footage of the murder. They were looking for a book."

"Which one?" Claire asked, looking up at Kate over her cup with a clear, focused expression.

"Does it make a difference?" Kate asked, curious. The change in her demeanour was stark.

"Of course it does. Some of those books… they're…well, they're valuable, and…" Claire sighed.

"And what?"

"Some of them are dangerous."

"Dangerous?" Kate was incredulous. How could a book be dangerous?

"You wouldn't understand, but yes, in the wrong hands, they can be dangerous."

"Right…" Kate wasn't sure what to make of that. What did she mean by dangerous? She sounded like someone from a horror film warning the rebellious teenage kids not to mess with things they didn't understand.

"Which book was it, Detective O'Connell?" Claire pressed again.

Kate was impressed that she'd remembered her name. She opened her notes to refresh her memory. "The Libre Exterious, I think it's called."

Claire blinked once, but her expression remained stony. "Makes sense. So, I take it they didn't get the book, then."

"Do you know where it is?" Nathan cut in.

Kate looked over at him, surprised that he'd spoken up.

"Of course. I know where all his books are, and that one is not at Alister's house."

"We guessed that. Where is it?" Nathan pressed.

"It's with Theadora Clement. She's another researcher who specialises in this area. He commissioned her on my advice."

"And where is Theadora?" Kate asked.

"I'll get you her address," Claire replied, standing up and retrieving a small notebook from a nearby drawer. "I hope she's okay. There was a lot of interest in that book."

"Oh?" Kate asked.

Claire sat back down. "I mean, that's not unusual, for a book of that calibre, but yes, it had generated more buzz than any of his last ten finds combined. I always told him to be careful. I wish he'd listened to me."

"You were aware of the kinds of people he traded with?" Nathan asked.

"Oh yeah, but I kept out of their way. He did business with some scary buggers, that's for sure. It's why I keep the door locked."

"Like who?" Kate asked.

Claire stopped hunting through her phone book and sat back. "Oftentimes it was difficult to say. It was just a feeling or a look they gave you that just screamed psychopath, you know? Some were very quiet. He had a few who'd only come at night, or always wore black, and sometimes, I could swear that when I looked at them..."

"What?" Kate asked, curious to know what she was thinking as a haunted look passed over her face. She seemed to shiver.

"No, it's nothing. Just my overactive imagination, you know?"

"Was there anyone recently? Anyone who seemed to worry Alister?" Nathan asked.

"No, I don't think so. He was a very relaxed man."

Nathan pulled out the printout from the security footage and showed her the pixelated face of the Dragon. "What about this man?"

Claire leaned in and examined the paper. "Is that the killer?"

"Do you recognise him?" Nathan asked again.

"No, I don't. But I didn't always see all of his clients."

"In answer to your question, yes, that was the man who killed him," Kate replied.

"Okay, thank you," she replied. "Oh, here it is. Yes. Theadora. She lives in Esher. She'd been visiting Alister quite a lot recently. All to do with this book, I think. Here you go, that's her address."

"Thank you, Claire. You've been most helpful."

"My pleasure. Come back anytime."

Kate stood and watched Nathan pick up another biscuit.

"I'll show you out," Claire said, making for the hallway. Kate grabbed a biscuit too and followed them out of the room.

Chapter 12

"How'd it go?" Kate asked.

"Fine," Rachel answered from the other end of the line. "He's a bit of a wheeler-dealer, but I didn't get the impression he would have done something like this. He didn't fit the body type of any of the men on the security footage either. Not only that, but he had an alibi for the night in question."

"Good."

"How about you?"

"Claire was interesting. An odd one, to be honest. She's old before her time and a little intense, but not a killer. She wasn't a match for anyone in the video, either. I don't think she was involved, even at an organisational level. So, what about Richard's relationship with Alister?"

"Not much more than a working one, I think. Richard has other people he represents, so it wasn't a terribly close relationship."

"Did you show him the picture of the Dragon?"

"Yeah, but he didn't recognise him."

"Alright, good job. What are you doing now?"

"Heading back to the station," Rachel replied. "We'll see if we can track down the fence Alister used. You?"

"Claire gave us another lead. Another researcher who apparently has the book that the gang is after. We're going to check it out."

"Sounds good. See you later."

"Bye," Kate replied, and the phone clicked off.

"No luck?" Nathan asked.

"Nope. Richard was a dead end. They're going to try and chase down the fence."

"Great."

"What was your impression of Claire?"

"She's not the killer," Nathan replied. "I mean, that's fairly obvious, as we have video of it, but I don't think she was involved."

"Why would she? She already has access to the books whenever she wants, so yeah, I can't see her wanting to kill Alister for them."

"What about his wealth, though? He's rich, she isn't…"

Kate nodded and sighed. "Yeah, I see that. Sure."

"Not convinced?"

"Not really,"

"No, me neither. Plus, there's also the biscuit issue."

Kate snorted. "I wondered about that. You didn't mention Bourbons or Rich Teas in your little speech to me."

"Don't forget the Custard Crèmes."

"Oh, well, absolutely. How could I forget about them?" Kate exclaimed.

"I saw you sneak one at the end."

"A girl's gotta eat." Kate smiled back at him.

"Not good dunkers, though," Nathan remarked. "You can always judge a good biscuit on how it dunks."

"So, why the hell are Hobnobs your favourite? They're terrible for dunking. They just break apart."

"You're clearly keeping them in the drink too long. There's an art to it, you know?"

"Apparently, I'm unaware of this dark art."

"Then, I'll have to teach you, young one," Nathan announced. "It's all about the timing. You need to find the sweet spot for each biscuit. Too short, and it's still too crunchy, too long, and you risk disaster."

"I had no idea it was such an in-depth topic," Kate replied, smiling.

"It's a key skill for a police officer to have, you know. Like the Americans and their doughnuts."

Kate rolled her eyes but giggled. "Let's just bring out all the stereotypes."

They chatted for a while longer as Nathan navigated the Surrey roads, eventually coming into the southern side of Esher. They turned onto a private side-road, complete with a white wooden gate to keep the ruffians out.

"She lives here?"

"That's the address," Nathan said, checking the sat-nav on his phone.

"Looks like we're dealing with another person with too much money."

"Too much?"

"Well, clearly. When I look at my bank account, I know I don't have enough, ergo, the people up this road have too much." She smiled smugly, enjoying the banter between them. She wasn't entirely serious, although she'd never say no to a pay rise.

"Nice logic there."

"I thought so," she replied, knowing it was flimsy as all hell.

They accelerated up the well-maintained brick-paved driveway, into a cul-de-sac where huge houses surrounded them. They were all sprawling affairs, with gated entrances and water features. Several cars had been parked up on the road, so Nathan pulled up behind one of them and turned the engine off. Kate climbed out and checked her notes, making sure they were heading onto the right property.

"This one," Kate said.

"It's another nice house," Nathan said as they walked through the open gate.

"Lovely, yeah," Kate agreed, feeling a little envious. "I wouldn't say no to living here."

"I bet you wouldn't."

Kate admired the well-kept garden and the gleaming Mercedes in the driveway, and couldn't help but let out a longing sigh. She liked her small studio flat. It was cosy and homely, but she didn't want to live there forever. She'd been saving as much as she could for months now, trying to build up a little nest egg so that one day, hopefully in the not too distant future, she could afford to put a deposit down on a house. She didn't need anything too big, but it would be wonderful to have a place of her own one day. Something she could do what she wanted with. She had plenty of ideas when it came to how she'd decorate it, she wasn't lacking in that department.

She let her mind drift over some of her ideas and dreams of what she'd do with a home of her own, allowing herself a moment of escapism as they approached the house.

She nearly walked into the back of Nathan when he stopped just short of the door.

"Ooops, sorry," she said, nearly falling over him. She frowned. "What's up?"

"Look," Nathan said, nodding at the door.

Kate looked ahead and saw the door was open, but not just open, it was buckled, and the frame had been partially pulled from its mounting.

"Shit," Kate hissed.

Nathan reached under his jacket and removed his gun. Kate felt her heartbeat quicken as she realised she needed to do the same. She'd never pulled her gun for real before, but she guessed there was a first time for everything.

Reaching under her jacket, she released the strap that kept the gun in its holster and drew her weapon. With another glance around, she gripped the slide and pulled it back, chambering a round, before gripping the gun in both hands and pointing it to the ground.

"What do you think?" Kate asked.

"I don't like it," Nathan replied, his voice low.

"Me neither," she replied, her stomach in her throat. Strangely, she felt a need to take control of the situation and decided to speak up. "I'll take point."

"Go for it."

Satisfied, Kate raised her weapon and approached the door, peering through the gap. Keeping her gun up, she reached out with her non-dominant hand and eased the door open. "Police!" she called out. "Armed Police."

Silence greeted her.

"We're coming in," she added and stepped through the door into the hallway beyond. At her feet, a solid, worn-looking metal battering ram lay on the floor, discarded after getting through the door, its job done.

As she took another step, she heard an engine rev loudly outside. Kate turned. In the road, a car, one of the ones that had been parked up, spun in a tight doughnut. Its tires squealing before it rocketed up the street, back the way they'd entered the short, dead-end road.

"Crap," Nathan said as he rushed outside and raised his gun, but the car was too far away. He cursed again and looked back at her.

A clatter of movement sounded inside the house.

Kate turned but saw nothing in the hallway. She looked back at Nathan. He'd heard it too and had moved back into the house, his gun up and ready.

"Go," he urged her.

Kate nodded and moved through the hallway. Something slammed in a room ahead, so Kate hustled forward into the doorway.

In an otherwise pristine kitchen, a woman lay on her back, her face bloody, but she was moving and moaning. Beyond her, a back door stood open.

Kate moved with urgency towards the woman, keeping her gun up, covering the room.

"Ngh... that way," the woman, who she guessed to be Theadora, gasped. She pointed towards the door.

"Go on," Nathan urged. "You're faster than I am. I'll watch her and call it in."

Kate nodded and bolted for the door. She slowed as she stepped out, checking her corners, only to spot a large man run into the bushes at the back of the garden.

"Hey!" Kate didn't think he'd stop by just shouting at him, but she did it anyway. "Armed Police, stop!"

He was out of sight.

Kate cursed and ran. She charged over the decking and onto the grass beyond, pumping her legs as fast as she could.

As she breached the tree line, she caught a glimpse of him ahead between the trees. Encouraged, she put on another burst of speed as adrenaline coursed through her body.

The man reached a six-foot fence and with a jump, hauled himself up and over it, glancing back.

It was him. The killer. She was sure of it.

No way. You're not getting away from me that easily.

Kate charged towards the fence, and at the last moment, leapt for the top of it. She got her arms on top and hauled herself up, catching sight of the man before he was blocked from her view again by another tree.

"Goddammit, no, you don't." Kate threw her leg up, pulled herself over, and fell to the ground. The landing was not the most graceful in the world, but she kept hold of her gun and felt proud of that, at least.

In that brief moment of quiet, she heard shouts ahead. A woman yelped and screamed. Kids called for their parents.

"Fuck, no way," she hissed. Energy flooded her veins and she set off again. Picking a gap between bushes, she sprinted through it. Branches ripped at her shirt and jacket, slapping her in the face.

Bursting out the other side, she found herself at the back of an even larger house. A family was beside their pool, enjoying the pleasant day. The wife hugged her kids close, the husband stood nearby.

"Armed Police," Kate called out. "Which way did he go?"

The man pointed. "Through there."

Kate followed his gesture and felt sure she spotted movement. She charged off again, crossing the garden in seconds and running between the trees on the far side. Ahead, she caught sight of the man again making for a wall.

Another one?

Kate braced herself as the man scaled it in moments before she could get a clear shot.

Kate piled on the speed again as he disappeared from view, pumping hard. Reaching the wall she scrambled up it, feeling sure she looked like a bloody idiot. Getting above the top of the wall, Kate saw a side street on the other side.

Commercial units and business buildings lined either side, and several people walked along the pavement.

"Ugh, come on," she grunted as she pulled herself over the wall and dropped to the pavement on the other side. Her landing was a little less messy this time, and she was on her feet quicker.

Tires screeched.

A car pulled to a stop at the end of the road and a door opened. It was the same car that had sped away from the house moments before.

"Police!" Kate bellowed again. "Armed Police, everyone down!" she shouted at the top of her lungs. She was nowhere near having a clean shot, though, as the man ran through pedestrians. Cursing, Kate ran, keeping her gun pointed down. "Move, get out of the way," she shouted as the man closed on the waiting car.

Kate ran up the road as people screamed and ran for cover. Most moved in sensible directions, but several didn't, getting in her way.

"Goddammit, MOVE!" She had seconds before he was in that car and gone.

Running towards the middle of the road to get a better angle, she planted her feet and aimed, putting her finger over the trigger. Beyond the car, on the other side of the street, people walked.

She didn't have a clear shot.

She watched in vain as the man dropped into the car and grabbed the door. He looked back at her and sensing she wouldn't shoot, paused and smiled at her.

He shut the door, and the car sped off.

Kate lowered her gun. "Shitting, pissing hell."

Chapter 13

The patrol vehicle pulled up in the cul-de-sac, alongside several other emergency vehicles that had arrived since they'd gotten to the scene.

She thanked the officer who'd given her a lift back around to the house and wandered inside, passing more uniformed police as she went. The SOCO's were already here, dusting the battering ram for prints. Wandering through, Kate eventually found Nathan sat at the kitchen table with the woman they'd found on the floor.

"You took your time," Nathan said with a smile.

"Had myself my own little crime scene just off the high street," Kate replied.

"What happened? I take it he got away?"

"Yeah," Kate replied with a sigh. "The car that booked it out of here picked him up. I just couldn't catch him and never really got a clear shot."

"You didn't fire your gun," Nathan replied. "That's a good thing."

Kate nodded and sighed. "I know."

Nearby, a paramedic was tending to the injured woman's wounds.

"Is that?"

"That's Theadora, yes," Nathan replied.

"Have you spoken to her?"

"Not yet, I've had my hands full," he said, raising them to show off the bloodstains on his cuffs where he'd helped the victim.

Kate nodded.

"Hey, gang."

Kate looked back to find DCI Dean approaching.

"Guv," Kate greeted him.

Nathan nodded. "Afternoon."

"He got away, then," he said. It wasn't a question.

"Yeah," Kate replied. "Sorry."

"Don't be. You did the right thing. You didn't have a shot, from what I hear, and you didn't take it. No one died. That's good."

"I know. I just wish I'd been able to stop him," Kate said.

"So do I, but the lives of innocents come first."

"I know."

"You'll have to fill in a report," he said.

"I will, don't worry."

"Good. Good work, detectives. Keep on it," the DCI said, and moved to talk to other people.

Nearby, at the other end of the table, the paramedic stepped away from Theadora. "You can talk to her now, if you want. I'll be back in a moment."

Kate nodded and sat down, looking over at Theadora. "Hey. How are you?"

"I'm okay, thanks," Theadora answered, and turned to Nathan. "Thank you for helping me."

"Anytime. Just doing my job."

She nodded. "If you'd not arrived when you did..."

"Don't think about that," Kate advised her. "What-ifs don't get you anywhere."

"Yeah, I know. Thanks."

"Theadora, is it?" Kate asked.

"Just Thea's fine," she answered.

"Okay, Thea. Do you know why this happened?"

She nodded. "They wanted the book. They killed Alister, right?"

Kate nodded. "That's right."

"They would have killed me, too."

"Probably."

Thea nodded. "I have it. He didn't get the book. It's still here. You're going to take it away, right?"

"We are," Nathan answered her.

Thea went to stand but cringed in pain.

"No, stop. You stay there, we can get the book in a moment. There's no rush."

"Okay," Thea replied.

"Do you know who that was, who hurt you?"

"Sorry, no," she replied, her voice strained from the pain she was in. "One of the interested parties, I'm guessing."

"Claire said Alister had lots of people interested in the book."

Thea nodded. "He did. People and organisations."

Kate looked over at Nathan and then back at Thea. "Like the Black Hand?"

"Yeah, they'd be interested in it," she answered.

"You know them, then?"

"I do. Not personally mind, but I know of them. I take it the people who did this, work for them?" She pointed to her face.

"That's our assumption," Kate replied.

"Figures. Seems like I've experienced their reputation first hand."

"You got off lightly," Nathan added.

"What were you doing with the book?" Kate inquired.

"Translating it mainly, also checking its authenticity and recording what's inside it. All pretty boring stuff. It's what we always do before we decide if we're going to sell it on."

"Were you?" Nathan asked.

"I don't know. Not anymore, though. You can take it, I don't want it."

"How did you know, Alister?" Kate asked.

"I only knew him by reputation, until Claire introduced me to him. She thought I might be able to help him with the book. I said I'd take a look at it, but I had no idea it would lead to this. Alister didn't deserve to die."

"What's the book all about?" Nathan asked.

"What's it about?"

"Yeah," Nathan pressed.

"It's... um. It's complicated."

"Try us," Kate replied.

"It's old, really old. It's a collection of works gathered down through the centuries, and it talks about... It's going to sound silly."

"Well, clearly the Black Hand doesn't think it's silly, not if they're willing to kill people over it."

Thea nodded. "It talks about distant realms. Like, worlds, or dimensions that are unlike anything here on earth or anywhere else. It talks about how to reach them and communicate with the... those who live there."

"What, like demons or something? Ghosts?"

"Worse."

Kate nodded slowly. It sounded like this woman had taken leave of her senses, quite frankly. She looked over at Nathan, who had been listening intently. She wondered if he believed Thea. It sounded like utter madness to her.

"And what do you think the Black Hand would want it for?" Nathan asked.

"Nothing good," Thea replied.

"Like?"

"Oh, God, I don't know. Maybe they want to try and summon something?"

"Okay, I think that's enough of that," Kate cut in, unable to proceed down this road any further. This was just crazy talk. "Shall we go and get the book?"

"Please do, I don't want it anywhere near me anymore," she answered as the paramedic returned.

"We're taking you in," the paramedic said. "I want to get you checked out properly."

"Okay," Thea replied and looked back at Kate and Nathan. "Thank you, the book's in my back office, back through the hallway and right."

Kate thanked her, and let Thea leave with the paramedic before she walked through the house with Nathan.

"You don't believe all that, do you?"

"Heh," Nathan said. "There are more things in heaven and earth, my dear."

"My dear? Are you patronising me by paraphrasing Shakespeare?"

"All I'm saying is, it's often better to keep an open mind. A sceptical mind, sure, but an open one."

"So you believe it?"

Nathan sighed. "I don't know what I believe. I've seen some crazy shit in my time that's difficult to explain so... Maybe?"

"Right. Well, don't you go summoning any demons or anything, alright? They might actually like Fig Rolls, then what would you do?"

Nathan snorted. "I'd feel vindicated."

"Ha! I bet you would."

They found their way into Thea's back office, and it was obvious which book was the Libre Exterious. It was set on a lectern beside Thea's desk, closed, but with sticky notes surrounding it. On the desk were scattered notes and diagrams both of the book itself, and of strange symbols that must be inside the book. There was a scattered pile of photos to one side too, showing the exterior and interior details of the book.

Kate ran her eyes over the photos of the pages and noted that some of the images appeared slightly distorted.

As she frowned at them, it was as if the images swam before her eyes. Light seemed to leak from some of the symbols in streaks and burn her retinas. She blinked, trying to banish the strange effect, and suddenly the photos were as she'd first seen them.

She looked up at Nathan. "Did you see...?"

"See? See what?"

Kate looked back at the perfectly normal photos and shook her head. "Nothing, it's nothing."

"We'd better gather all this up. Some of it might be useful," Nathan suggested."

Kate agreed, fished a pair of gloves from her coat pocket, slipped them on, and set to work. As she pulled together some of the photos, she had a feeling that someone was watching her. It was as if eyes were burrowing into the back of her head. She turned, but Nathan wasn't paying her any attention. Instead, her eyes slid down to the book, and she had the feeling that it was somehow…

No, that's just silly.

She shook her head again, banishing such thoughts.

Books don't look at you.

Chapter 14

"So, this is it, the book that these guys were after?" Damon walked over to where Nathan had placed the tome on the table in the Incident Room.

The book itself was huge, easily forty centimetres tall and thirty wide when closed. It was bound in badly worn leather with metal clasps and corners that were dinged and scratched. On the cover, a faded image of a circle sat in the centre. It had lines radiating out from it, leading to other, smaller circles all around it.

Here, in the modern décor of the Horsley Station, the book looked decidedly out of place, and its age felt even greater. Damon cooed over it, leaning in to get a closer look and gently running his fingers over the edges.

"This really is a thing of beauty," he said without taking his eyes off of it. "You got it at Theadora's?"

"Yeah. She didn't want it anymore. She insisted we take it."

"I'm not surprised, after what she went through," Rachel said.

Kate nodded. "She was pretty badly beaten."

"I heard you went all Wonder Woman?" Rachel asked her.

Kate laughed. "I guess you could say that. Tried chasing him down, but he was too fast with too much of a head start."

"You're sure it was him?" Zafar asked.

"Positive. It was the killer. The bald man. I'd recognise him anywhere."

"Mind if I have a look inside?" Damon asked, pointing to the book.

"Just be careful with it," Nathan said.

Damon nodded and returned to the book, where he gently levered open the cover, revealing cracked, coffee stain-coloured pages, covered in tight writing surrounding geometric symbols and sketches of demonic faces.

Kate found herself strangely drawn to the contents of the book and watched carefully as Damon slowly turned the pages one at a time, revealing ever more horrific imagery.

"Kate!"

"Huh?" She looked up to see Nathan, Dion, and Rachel all looking at her. "What? I'm right here."

"We know, we called your name several times."

"Oh, did you?" She felt confident she'd have heard them if they did. "Sorry."

"It's okay," Rachel replied. Kate turned to glance back at the book, only to find Nathan had stepped sideways and was now blocking her view of it.

Kate smiled at him.

He smiled back.

"I was just saying," Dion said, "we have CCTV footage of the getaway car. I've pulled the plate, but it's a stolen one. So probably a dead end."

Kate nodded. "Okay, good. Thanks. See if you can trace it anyway, you never know your luck."

"Will do."

"The SOCO's pulled a tyre track from the road too, so we might be able to cross-reference it. So keep an eye out for that. I'm sure they'll send up whatever they have."

Dion nodded.

"So, what did Theadora say this book was all about?" Damon asked.

"She said it contained detailed information about other realms or dimensions," Nathan replied, sounding like an authority on the subject.

"I see," Damon replied. "And did she speculate on why the Black Hand might want it?"

"She said they'd likely use it to try and summon something," Nathan answered.

"Makes sense," Damon replied. "Look at the other two killers you've dealt with that had links to the Hand—all their killings had ritualistic trappings, they used similar markings and such at the kill sites, and they seemed to believe they were contacting some kind of higher power—all common links between them."

"Not at Alister's killing, though," Kate replied. "There were none of the usual markers at the scene."

"And yet," Damon continued, "this case feels like it has stronger links to the Black Hand than the others. They were hunting down a book that would help them do more of these kinds of killings, but with a greater focus than before, perhaps?"

"What do you know about this Black Hand?" Nathan asked.

Damon sat back. "They're a secretive group. We don't know much about their current leadership, but we're fairly sure they started as a splinter group of the Serbian terror organisation that kicked off the first World War by killing Ferdinand."

"And this group came from that one?" Kate asked.

"We've heard differing stories and theories," Damon replied. "But that is the most common, or most popular one. Apparently, a member of the Serbian group broke away and started his own organisation after coming into possession of occult knowledge. Over the years, they traded in that knowledge, and became quite powerful."

"Do we know who that founder was?"

"The name I hear most is Andrej Zorić, but that's only rumour."

"So he'd be what, over a hundred now?"

"I don't believe he's around anymore, from what I've heard. The Hand suffered several setbacks in recent years that caused it to go through a change of leadership. We know very little about this new Black Hand, other than it's a much smaller affair compared to the global organisation that it used to be. Now, it seems to be based around here, in the UK."

"Lucky us," Kate replied sarcastically.

"That's good, though," Damon protested. "We need to stop the group from growing and becoming something much bigger and harder to take down. We have a chance to stop them with fewer resources than we'd need to take down a global organisation."

"Well, we'll certainly do our best," Nathan replied.

Kate nodded. "If we put all this magical mumbo-jumbo to one side for a moment, what I know is that we have a group of people who think they are above the law and who are killing people to get their way. I'm all for stopping them from hurting anyone else, and anything we can do to stop that, is fine with me."

"Hey, who wants pizza?" Rachel asked.

"Are you buying?" Nathan asked.

"Piss off... sir."

Kate laughed. "We'll all pitch in."

"Awesome," Dion replied. "Mine's a meat feast!"

Chapter 15

Kate walked along a cold, angular corridor of smooth concrete. It was dark and cool to the touch beneath her bare feet.

Ahead, the shadowy hallway ended, and dim light streamed in and splashed over the floor a short distance ahead. Behind her, the tunnel faded into murky darkness.

She pressed on, moving towards the light at the end of the corridor. She could see beyond, into what appeared to be a huge open space.

She pressed on, padding steadily up the tunnel, brushing her hands against the smoothed-out stone walls.

Her fingers brushed over indentations. She pulled her hand back to see great slashes across the wall as if powerful claws had cut into the stone.

Kate recoiled from the markings, but as she stared at them, she felt sure she heard a shuffling, clicking movement off to her right.

Peering into the darkness, there didn't seem to be anything there, but she couldn't be sure.

Returning her attention to the way ahead, she pressed on to the end of the corridor. Around her, the walls and ceiling just stopped, but the floor continued as a long platform, which stretched out over a black void below.

Stepping out, she could see the corridor she'd been in had been a hole cut into a vast wall that extended as far as she could see, fading away into shadow and mists. All around her, more distant holes and ledges were cut into that wall. Stairwells spiralled up and down. Bridges, like the walkway she was standing on, stretched out into the darkness, crossing to another vast wall ahead, bridging the gap.

Shivering, she wrapped the light, dirty sheet that was her only clothing around her in a vain effort to stay warm.

Staying near the wall, she held it as she peered over the side of the walkway. There were more bridges and platforms far below. Much too far to jump.

The sound of something moving came from the shadows again.

Kate stepped back from the tunnel. She thought she caught a glimpse of something flash or move in the gloom.

Was she imagining things?

She stepped back in fear as her heart thundered in her chest. Her foot nearly went over the edge of the walkway.

Pulling herself back, she dropped into a crouch.

Something shiny, like a huge insect's carapace, shifted in the shadows.

Kate got up and looked around. She could see others. People on the other platforms, walking in this nightmare realm.

"Hey!" Her voice echoed through the vast space, bouncing off the walls, but no one seemed to hear her.

The thing in the tunnel hissed, and something, a leg maybe, shifted.

There was nothing for it, she was alone. Turning, Kate ran along the walkway, her rags trailing behind her. The thing hissed again. She glanced back and saw a horror from her deepest nightmares rushing after her.

"No. I can't die. Not here. No." Ahead, the walkway ended.

It just stopped.

There was nowhere to go. The thing was coming.

There was nothing for it, she wouldn't let that thing end her life. She would be the master of her own destiny. She would choose when and how she died.

With her heart in her throat, she jumped.

Darkness rose up and enveloped her.

Kate awoke with a start, her eyes snapping open in the dim morning light of her flat.

Her heart pounded in her chest, as she gasped for breath. Her covers were all over the place and half on the floor.

Her mouth was dry. She needed a drink.

Sitting up, she checked her phone. It was only just gone five-thirty in the morning. Kate rubbed her eyes and yawned before standing up and padding over to her kitchenette and pouring a glass of water.

It was cool in her mouth, her body rejoicing at the feeling of the life-giving liquid. The images and feelings from the nightmare faded, and she found it difficult to remember exactly what she'd been dreaming about. Something about falling?

As her heart rate slowed and her breathing returned to normal, she caught sight of another letter on the floor near the door, and her blood froze.

Another one.

Taking a breath, Kate placed her glass on the counter and crossed her apartment. It was the same as all the others, with her name written on the front in that familiar spidery handwriting. Inside was a simple note.

Flat 1. Come Now.

Kate frowned at it, wondering what it meant. Flat one was Francine's place. For a moment, she wasn't sure what the best thing to do was. What would be waiting for her downstairs? Had he killed her? Was he in there, holding Francine captive?

A feeling of urgency grew inside her. She grabbed her keys and stepped out of her apartment into the short corridor. It was quiet.

Taking several slow, careful steps, she moved up the corridor to the stairs, trying not to make the floorboards creak under her weight. Reaching the top of the stairs, she edged out and peered down.

The entrance hallway was quiet. It was still early, and in the morning twilight, the shadows were deep. There was no one down there, though.

Looking back around the corridor, she made sure she was alone and took the first few steps down the stairs. She couldn't hear anything to suggest someone was in the building.

That didn't mean no one was, of course.

She was about to take another step when she realised she was still in her nightshirt with its loose neck that drooped over one shoulder it was so stretched.

Hardly the best clothing to be wearing to take on an intruder.

For a moment, she considered returning to her flat and putting some clothes on. Looking back down, she noticed Francine's door wasn't closed.

Kate frowned.

Curiosity getting the better of her, she sneaked down the remaining stairs and into the entrance hall. The area was devoid of life, but her focus was on Francine's door, which was indeed, ajar.

Manipulating her keys in her hand, she held them in such a way that several jutted out between her fingers, making them into an improvised weapon. Feeling a little better about things, she reached out and pushed the door open.

Francine's apartment stood empty and quiet. Kate moved inside, looking back and forth, checking behind the door and all around, but there was no one here. Pushing the door to behind her, she walked deeper inside.

"Hello?" she said, keeping her voice low.

Kate heard a muffled squeak from her right. Turning to the kitchen, she squinted into the darkness, but there was nothing there. The sound was strange, though. Like it was both distant, but not. It had a curious feel to it, as if the lower frequencies were missing.

She heard it again. Where was it coming from?

Taking another step, she caught sight of movement in the dim light. There was a tablet on the countertop with a moving image on it. Shifting around for a better view, Kate gasped.

It was a video feed of Francine, tied to a chair with a gag tied around her face. She stared at the camera, her eyes wet from the tears she'd shed. She tried to say something, but very little came through.

"Kate, welcome! So glad you could join us."

"What have you done?" Kate blurted out.

"Really? I would have thought that was obvious, Kate."

Gritting her teeth, she didn't answer. He was right, it was a stupid question.

"Cat got your tongue?" He laughed. "Oh, no. He can't, can he? He's buried in the garden."

"You're a monster," Kate spat.

The man laughed. "Perhaps."

"What do you want?" Kate was in no mood for a verbal sparring match.

"I would have thought that was fairly obvious by now. Come on Kate, think. What do you have that I want? Hmm?"

"I… I don't know," she answered, thinking through the various items of her aunt's that she kept in a box upstairs.

"Think Kate, think."

"My aunt's phone?" she guessed.

The man laughed heartily. "Kate, dearest. I have absolutely no interest in your dead aunt's crap. Seriously, you disappoint me. I thought you'd have joined the dots by now."

Her mind suddenly made the connection. It was an idea she'd already had, but it had evaded her until that moment. "The book."

"Bingo! We have a winner. Give her a round of applause. My word, Kate that took far too long for you to get. Are you sure you're cut out to be a detective?"

"You want me to get you Alister's book."

"The Liber Exterious, yes. That one."

"But, I can't do that."

"I don't want to hear excuses, Kate. I want results."

"You're a part of the Black Hand."

"Kate, focus. You need to put your limited brainpower into thinking how you're going to get me that book. That needs to be your sole focus. I want that book."

"And if I don't?"

"Oh, you want me to spell it out for you, do you? Well, alright, I'll make it clear. Either you get me that book, or Francine here will die a very long, very painful death. Not only that, but the world will know about your sordid history. Your life will be over, Kate. You'll be fired from the police force and you'll be a criminal. Have you got that? Is that clear enough for you?"

"Crystal."

"Good. Now, I think you have a job to do. Nice nightshirt, by the way. Shows off your legs. Yum."

"Piss off."

"Be nice, Kate. Wouldn't want me to hurt Franny here, would you? Now, of course, I've seen a little bit more of you than what you've got on display today. You know about the videos, don't you? Hmm? I really do have some quite choice moments from your life over the past year or so. They make for some nice viewing on those lonely nights."

Kate grimaced, her stomach twisting with revulsion. She didn't like to think about what he was watching from the videos Wilson Hollins had saved of her. With a deep breath, she banished those thoughts to the back of her mind and focused on what he wanted her to do. "This isn't going to be easy."

"Nothing in life ever is."

Kate frowned, wondering how the hell she was going to get the book out of a building full of police without anyone knowing about it. "If I'm caught, you won't get the book."

The man sighed. "Alright, as you've clearly dressed to impress me, how about this? I'll message you later today when we're ready. Once we are, and you're in the station, let us know, and we'll provide a distraction. Okay?"

Kate sighed. "Okay, fine, I'll see what I can do."

"You'd better, otherwise, Fran will not have a good day."

Chapter 16

Arriving at work, Kate stepped out of her car and looked up at the building, seeing it in a very different light.

Yesterday, it had just been her place of work. A friendly building where people she liked gathered to try and make her little corner of the planet a safer place for everyone to live.

It was a place she enjoyed coming. A place where her friends worked. A place she felt welcome.

This morning, it felt like enemy territory. All those doors and security measures that helped keep her safe, were now obstacles for her to overcome.

As she walked in, she saw her colleagues in a different light too. They were potential problems, or even enemies now. They could stop her and foil her plan.

They could unwittingly cause an innocent woman to be killed, just by doing their job. She felt distinctly uncomfortable as she walked through the familiar building and up into the open-plan office of the Murder Team.

It was like stepping into the lion's den. She felt sure that everyone who looked at her knew that she was up to no good. It was as if she were carrying a huge sign that said 'acting suspiciously' in big blinking letters.

She hated feeling like this and hated her aunt's killer for causing it. He was an utter monster, there was no doubt about that. But what could she do? Telling anyone not only risked her job, but risked the investigation. She could be viewed as compromised, and worst of all, it risked Francine's life.

As far as she could see, there was no way around it. She'd just have to try to find a way to get the book out of the building, but she knew that would be easier said than done.

Moving into the Incident Room, Nathan looked up at her.

"Morning," he greeted her.

"Hey," she replied and looked around as she dumped her bag into her usual chair. Dion sat at one of the computers, turning it on as he settled in, and Damon was already buried deep in the book. Reading what he could and making notes as he went.

There was no way she could casually ask to borrow the book without looking suspicious, especially if she then walked out of the building with it.

She sighed, wondering if this was a lost cause.

"Here you go." Nathan held out a file to her, tapping her arm with it.

"Hmm?" Kate said, looking at it. "What's this?"

"The Sandford Case. I had Debby make a copy of it for you. We're going to speak with him at the prison later today, so I thought we should both familiarise ourselves with the particulars, see if there are any links to the recent cases.

Kate nodded and took the file. "Yeah, alright," she answered, glad for a distraction from her current predicament.

Clearing a space on her desk, she flicked the file open and started to go through it. "Don't you remember the case?" she asked.

"I wish," he replied. "My memory isn't what it used to be. It's why I write everything down these days."

Kate smiled, nodded, and shrugged, returning her attention to the file and began reading it. She made her way through the report and the overview of the case but found nothing that linked Sandford to their current case or to the Dragon, so she started reading up on Sandford himself in much more detail, digging through the research that Nathan and his team had done years ago. The names of businesses and people who were linked with Sandford seemed endless. Ronald Ware, Alexia Bancroft, Jon Parsons, they were just meaningless names, and none of them seemed to have a link to any of their cases. She was over an hour and a half in, and totally consumed by the task when a familiar business name suddenly came to light.

"Oh, hang on," Kate said, before finishing the section and looking up at Nathan. "Look here."

"What's up?" Nathan asked as he scootered over on his wheeled office chair.

"Look. Recognise that name?"

"Huh! The Bellrose Modelling Agency. Sandford had links to it?"

"That's right. As part of the work he was doing for a client, he did a little bit of work with the agency. Not much, but there's a clear link."

"Interesting. So he did a little work for the agency that some of Solomon's victims worked for. I think that's a little more than a coincidence."

"I agree," Kate said, as she kept reading. A little further down, she came across another link. "Well shit. Not only did he do a little work with them, he actually dated one of their models briefly. Want to know which one?"

Nathan frowned at her. "It's one of Solomon's victims, isn't it? Which one?"

"Isabelle Trask," Kate confirmed. "The one who had her face caved in inside the abandoned house."

"Shit, why didn't I remember that? Who did that research?"

"Hang on," Kate replied and flicked back to the first page of this collection of papers. "Sam Mason," Kate replied. "In fairness, these things weren't really relevant to your case at the time."

"Still, I feel bad that I didn't remember it. Shit. How long ago did they date?"

"Several years, according to this…" Kate replied.

"She might have been underage," Nathan suggested.

"Oh, yeah, maybe. Hang on, let me work it out… Okay, I think she was about sixteen, maybe seventeen at the time."

"Okay, right on the borderline then."

"He'd have been in his late thirties, early forties maybe?" Kate worked out.

"They can't have had much in common," Nathan said, screwing his face up.

"I doubt he was dating her for the scintillating conversation."

"No, probably not."

"So, what does this mean for us, and this case? Are they linked? Did Sandford have links to the Black Hand as well?"

"I have no idea," Nathan admitted. "But it's suspicious."

"Was the agency involved? Do they have links to the Hand? This probably bears doing some more investigation, but I know one thing."

"What's that?"

"I'd like to speak with Isabelle's parents again, see if they remember her dating Sandford."

Chapter 17

"Good morning, detectives," Lucy Trask said in greeting as she opened the door to them. She looked quite different than when Kate had last seen her. Their previous visit had been right after the death of their daughter, and Lucy had been distraught.

Today, she was wearing a little makeup and welcomed them with more level and measured tones.

"Please, come in. It's good to see you again."

"Thank you, Mrs Trask."

"Please, call me Lucy. So, you said on the phone you wanted to ask us something about Izzy?" Lucy led them into their lounge where Mr Trask stood at the window waiting. He turned.

"Morning, Detectives."

"Morning," Nathan replied.

"Hello, Mr Trask," Kate said. "Yes, that's right, but it's in relation to a different case."

"What about the case against Solomon? How's that going?" he asked.

"Slowly, as always. These things take time, but rest assured, we will do our best for you. The evidence against him is compelling, to say the least."

"Still nothing on Adam Archer?"

"No, I'm afraid not," Kate replied, remembering his intense dislike of the photographer who'd taken provocative images of their murdered daughter.

"I still think you should look into him more. There's something..."

"Ted," Lucy cut in. "Will you just leave it."

"But..."

"But nothing, Ted. For the love of God, just drop this silly vendetta against that photographer. There's nothing there."

"I'm sorry," he replied, suitably chastised.

"You're always sorry, Ted. Always. But you just won't leave it, will you? Why can't you just remember Izzy for who she was, and forget this stupid need to get back at Adam." Lucy sighed. Ted didn't answer. A few seconds later, Lucy looked up. "I'm sorry. Please, go on, Detective."

"Look, I'm sorry to come around, dredging all of this up again. I know it's tough. At least you have each other."

Lucy grunted.

Kate decided to ignore it. "Does the name Sandford Barret mean anything to you?"

"Sandford?" Lucy asked.

"That's right. It appears that Isabelle knew him several years back when she was maybe sixteen or seventeen?"

"No, sorry. I don't remember any of her friends having that name."

"Aaah, well, he won't have been a school friend or anything. He would have had connections to the Bellrose Modelling Agency, and will have been around thirty-nine, or forty at the time."

"Um, no, sorry. The name doesn't ring any bells."

"How did they know each other?" Ted asked.

"We think they dated briefly."

"What?" Ted asked. "You're kidding me?"

"Dated?" Lucy sounded sceptical. "Oooh, no. She never had a boyfriend at sixteen. Not a serious one."

"Was she modelling by then?" Nathan asked.

"She started at sixteen, yes."

Ted cut in. "Are you saying some perverted forty-year-old was seeing my baby girl?"

"Well, we can't be sure. Not really," Kate said.

"Who is this Sandford, anyway?" Ted asked.

"He was the subject of a murder investigation several years ago. He killed his mistress."

"Oh, God," Lucy and Ted both exclaimed at the same time.

Ted added, "And where is he now?"

"He's behind bars and won't be out for a long time," Nathan replied. "But it seems to be linked to our current case, and during our investigation we discovered this link to Isabelle, and thought it best to follow it up."

"Well, he can stay there, for all I care," Ted replied.

"So, you don't know a Sandford, you've never heard the name?" Kate asked to clarify.

"No, sorry. No idea," Lucy answered.

Ted sighed. "Nothing, no."

"I'm sorry we couldn't be more help," Lucy added.

Chapter 18

Nathan pulled up in the car park and turned off the engine. "Have you been here before?"

Kate shook her head. "No, I can't say I've ever had the pleasure."

"You're not missing much," Nathan replied. "I'm fairly sure it'll be the low point of your day."

Kate smiled and climbed out of the car. The car park was surprisingly busy, with plenty of cars parked up side by side.

Buttoning up her jacket, she walked with Nathan around towards the front entrance of High Down Prison, a category two male prison. They were just south of Sutton, in Surrey.

"So, he didn't make it into a category one, then?"

"Not many of those in the country," Nathan replied.

"Hmm. So, what are we expecting from this meeting? Is he even going to talk to us?"

"That, I do not know," Nathan replied. "I very much doubt he's forgiven me for putting him away."

"So, this might be a dead-end?"

"It's worth a shot. He might be the key to finding out who this Dragon guy is. He must have known him if he got him to break into my house and attack me."

"Makes sense," Kate agreed.

Kate followed Nathan up to the main entrance of the prison. The building's tall, weather-worn walls stretched off to either side of the entrance with its beige, almost-pink brick and mirrored windows. It was a severe, brutal-looking building, similar to Horsley Station in a way. But where Horsley Station projected strength, here there was a bleakness and hopelessness to the building that Kate didn't like.

Walking in, they were greeted by the staff and identified themselves. They filled in some visitor forms and surrendered their gear before being told to sit and wait.

The chairs were cold, solid, and screwed down, all of which made them incredibly uncomfortable as Kate sat and watched others going about their business.

A short time later, a prison guard walked in and spoke with the receptionist, who pointed over to them.

"Heads up," Kate said and stood as the man walked over.

"Officers," he said in greeting and shook their hands.

"Morning," they both greeted him.

"So, you're here to see Sandford?"

"That's right. He may have information that could help us with our current case," Nathan answered.

"Alright, well let's get you in, and we'll bring him to you."

The guard led them out through a gate and across a small courtyard. In the next building, they were shown to a table in the centre of an empty room that was part of the visitor's centre.

"Make yourselves comfortable," the guard suggested. "I'll bring him over."

The table and chairs were secured to the floor and Kate did her best to make herself comfortable.

It was a losing battle, but she hoped she wouldn't be here long anyway. Being inside a male prison was something of a daunting experience. She knew these walls held some quite nasty people, and she couldn't shake the idea of how horrible it would be to get caught here during a riot or something, where they were unable to get out. The idea made her shiver.

As they waited, other guards came and went, until eventually, the far door opened and the guard walked in with Sandford.

The man took one look at Nathan and his face fell. "Oh, fuck off. You again? What the hell did I do to deserve this?"

"Good morning, Sandford," Nathan said, sitting back.

"Piss off." He turned to the guard. "Do I have to speak to him?"

"Just sit down and listen to the man, alright?" the guard suggested.

With a grunt and a sigh, Sandford did as the guard asked, and dropped into one of the seats opposite, his cuffs clinking as he moved.

"Got yourself a pretty new partner then, Halliwell?"

"I'm DC O'Connell," Kate said.

He cocked his head to one side. "Pleasure, I'm sure." His reply was laced with sarcasm. "How much for a blow job?"

Kate did her best to hide her shock but felt sure she'd failed miserably.

Nathan smiled and leant forward. "You can be as obnoxious as you like, Sandford, but we're here to ask you some questions and we won't be leaving until we're satisfied."

"Wonderful," Sandford replied. "What about my satisfaction? Hmm?"

"What do you want?" Nathan asked. Kate saw where Nathan was going with this. Treat him nice, and maybe he'd open up.

"A beer?"

Nathan raised his eyebrows.

"Alright, alright. A coke, and a Yorkie."

Nathan turned to one of the guards in the room. "Can you see what you can do?"

The guard sighed and stepped out, returning moments later to say they were on it.

"There, we'll see what we can get you. Now, I have some questions for you."

"I ain't answering shit from you."

"What about from me?" Kate cut in.

"Depends what the question is, babe." He licked his lips.

Kate looked over at Nathan, who sat back and silently urged her to continue.

"We'd like you to identify someone for us."

"Is that right? Well, I ain't identifying anyone until I get my stuff."

Kate sighed and sat back while Sandford crossed his arms and looked at the ceiling. Minutes later, the guard returned with a plastic cup of coke, and a Boost Bar.

"I said a Yorkie," Sandford protested.

"It's that or nothing," the guard replied.

Sandford sighed. "Fine." He took a sip of his drink and opened the chocolate bar. After a bite, he smiled and looked back at her. "Okay, shoot."

Kate nodded and pulled out the printout with the Dragon's face on it. She unfolded it and placed it on the table.

"You know this man."

Sandford looked down at the image. He screwed his mouth up as he peered at it, and then sat back. "Do I?"

"You do. Several years ago, you got him to break into Nathan's house and assault him."

"Oh, yeah," he laughed. "I forgot you had your face broken by some random thugs," he said to Nathan with a smile. "No idea how that happened. Aah yes, those were happy times."

Nathan remained silent beside her.

"So, you remember the incident?" Kate asked.

"I remember Halliwell getting his ass handed to him."

"By this man."

"If you say so, lady."

"We know you hired him to do it," Kate pressed.

"Oh, do you? Are you sure about that? Because I believe that was never proven."

"But you did, didn't you?"

"That was a long time ago, I'm not sure I remember that far back. It's all a mess."

"What's his name, Sandford? Just give us a name."

"But I don't know his name. This is the first I've ever seen him."

"Bullshit," Nathan cut in. "You know exactly who it is. You sent this thug to kill me and my wife…"

"And what about my wife, huh? You destroyed my marriage. You destroyed my life! You did that!"

"No, Sandford, you did that to yourself when you had an affair and then killed your mistress. That was when your life ended, and it had nothing to do with me. I was just the poor bastard that had to clean up your mess."

"Piss off. I ain't talking to you. No way. Guard! Guard. Get me out of here." A guard approached and led Sandford out, leaving them in the room with the guard who'd originally met them in reception.

"That was impressive. He really doesn't like you," the guard said.

"No, he doesn't."

"Did you get what you needed?"

"Nowhere close," Kate replied but could see Nathan was deep in thought. "What are you thinking?"

They got up and followed the guard out of the room. "I'm not sure, but, I'm wondering about Sandford's wife."

"You think she might be able to help?"

"Who knows. Maybe? I think she's been given a new identity though, so we'll have to see if we can get permission to see her."

Chapter 19

Seeing the inside of High Down seemed to have a more significant impact on Kate than she had bargained for. She'd seen prisons before and was well aware of the conditions that many of them were in. But this one just seemed to set off her anxiety more than any of the others had previously.

She doubted it was the prison itself, it was more the circumstances that she found herself in. It was probably the worst day for her to visit a prison, and remind herself what she could be in for if she was caught sabotaging their case, or should the details of her past come to light.

She spent most of the journey back in silence as she wondered if there was any way for her to somehow save her neighbour from this maniac, and not destroy her own life in the process.

As they neared the station, her phone buzzed in her lap. She picked it up without thinking and opened the message.

'We're ready. Francine is depending on you. Say when...'

Kate's breath caught in the back of her throat and for a long moment, she struggled to inhale anything. Her heart hammered in her chest so hard she could actually feel it. It was as if her whole body was shaking from the force of it beating, sending her blood and adrenaline pumping through her body.

She closed her phone and sat perfectly still in the passenger seat, while her mind raced with thoughts and possibilities. How on earth was she going to do this? What was the distraction going to be? Would she be caught? Would she be going to prison in a few short days? Was there any way out of this?

She couldn't focus on the case, the car, their journey, or anything else. She was consumed by the sheer, mind-numbing terror of what would happen in the next few hours.

"I'm going to make some phone calls," Nathan said.

Kate jumped. "What?"

"Calls. I'm going to make some calls."

"Why?" she asked, suddenly terrified they would be calls about her.

"To see if we can see Sandford's wife?"

"Oh. Yeah, of course." She felt silly and even worse, she felt suspicious.

"Are you alright?"

"Yeah, fine. I'm fine."

"Are you sure? Because you're acting a little strange."

"Me? No. It's nothing. Just, um… You know…"

"No, not really," Nathan replied.

"Oh, um. Like, lady's problems…"

Nathan blinked. "Oh, okay."

Kate breathed easier. She should have thought of that earlier.

"Yeah, got them bad today, you know?" She put her hand to her pelvis and pretended to be in pain.

"Not really," he answered. "Do you want the rest of the day off?"

"No!"

"Okay..." he answered with a squeak, raising his hands in surrender. She immediately felt bad for snapping at him.

"Sorry. No, I need to work. Keeps my mind off things."

Nathan stared at her for a beat. "Alright. Well, I'm going in," he said with a smile. Kate noticed they'd stopped and were in the station's car park.

"Sure, yeah, um. I'm coming."

She stepped out the car and looked around the car park, wondering where her aunt's killer was.

She spotted her car parked a short distance away. If she could just get the book into her car, maybe she could get it away from the station, and deliver it to wherever her aunt's killer wanted it.

Surely, it wouldn't be too difficult to get it to her car. If the distraction was a good one, she might just be able to sneak it out. She'd be able to come up with some sort of excuse from there. Maybe if she got it out, she could fake being beaten up or something.

She sighed. One step at a time.

Just get the book out of the station.

She walked inside and took a long look around the main office. It was actually reasonably empty today for a change. Nathan sat at his desk on his phone with his back to her.

Nearby, DI Sam Mason and DS Tommy Taylor were in, working at their computers, and apart from a few others scattered around, that was it. Most of the desks were empty.

"Everything alright, Thelma?" Sam asked her from nearby, a smart grin on his face.

"Just checking if my 'Louise' is around, and he is," she replied with a snarky smile.

She didn't wait for a reply and walked over to the Incident Room and looked inside.

Empty.

The book sat on the table where Damon had been working on it. His notes were all around his workspace, but he wasn't there.

Perfect, she thought and grabbed her phone.

'Now,' she tapped in and sent the message as she walked into the Incident Room.

The next few moments seemed to drag on forever. Each second crawled by like an arthritic snail, as Kate dreaded

145

someone walking in moments before the distraction happened, causing her problems.

When were they going to do this? What were they going to do? Would anyone get hurt? Kate felt her stomach sink. Would it be that kind of distraction? Would they hurt anyone, or kill anyone?

Would she be able to live with herself if someone died for this?

A series of loud, rapid-fire bangs reverberated through the building.

Gunfire.

She'd heard enough of that recently to know exactly what it was.

Kate ducked on instinct, dropping to the floor. She heard distant glass shatter, as people shouted and screamed. More gunfire. Looking up, people were running, charging past the door.

Kate could only stare through into the office, her hands violently shaking as she struggled to comprehend what was going on. This was England. Sleepy Surrey. Gun battles didn't happen here.

What on earth had she gotten herself mixed up in?

She couldn't say how long she crouched there, paralysed with fear. She had caused this. She had asked for a distraction. What on earth did she think was going to happen? This was a powerful organisation who had no respect for the law and didn't value human life. Of course, they were going to hurt people. It was obvious.

"Aaagh," Kate grunted, running her hands through her hair. "Get it together. Francine, think of Francine," she muttered to herself and stood up, her fists clenched. She could still hear shouting, but the gunfire seemed to have stopped.

Kate grabbed the book, held it close, and stepped to the door. Her nerves were a scrambled mess. The office outside was almost entirely empty. She spotted a few distant heads popping up above tables, but they weren't part of their case.

Crucially, she couldn't see Nathan. Had he run out of the office on hearing the gunfire? She could only hope so.

It was now or never.

Steeling herself, she walked briskly towards the main door and looked out through the glass. A couple of people she didn't recognise walked by. She stepped out. It looked like the distraction happened at the front of the building.

Good, her car was at the back. Turning, she made for the door to the emergency stairs, where she stopped and looked around. No one seemed to have spotted her. She took a deep breath and walked into the stairwell, she was nearly there.

Just down here, out the rear entrance and across the car park.

She stepped onto the first flight of stairs, and Nathan appeared walking up towards her.

Kate stopped. He hadn't looked up.

She turned and without looking back, walked back through the door into the corridor. She saw Sam Mason through the glass in the main office talking with DS Taylor.

She couldn't go back. The lifts would take too long. The main stairs were so far away, and there were too many people.

"Kate?"

She turned. Nathan was in the door to the stairs.

"What are you doing?" He looked down at the large book she clutched to her chest.

"Nothing, just taking a walk," she replied and made for the stairwell door, hoping to slip past. She daren't look at him. If she looked into those eyes of his, he'd know, and she didn't know if she could hold it all together.

His hand shot out in front of her.

"Wait, where are you taking the book?"

Kate looked down as if she'd only just realised she was carrying it. She tried to say something. Anything. She needed to say something. But there was nothing there.

Why couldn't she come up with an excuse? Why was her mind just not working? It was an easy question, but it felt like he'd asked her some kind of impossible math problem.

Taking her gently by the arm, Nathan turned and ushered her into a side room. It was a smallish office and was currently unoccupied. Nathan put his back to the glass door to stop anyone else from coming in and stared right at her.

"Spill it," he said.

"Spill it? Spill what? I'm just, I'm not..." Looking up, her eyes locked with his. She wasn't fooling him at all.

She tried to speak again. Instead, a racking sob escaped her lips and her eyes watered. She didn't know what to say. Her mind flailed around for words. Any words. But nothing would come. She was out of excuses, and the idea that people might have died in this building because of her was suddenly too much.

Dropping the book, she buried her head in her hands and let the tears come.

Nathan's arms wrapped around her and held her close.

"It's okay," he reassured her. "We can work through this. I can help. Just tell me what's going on."

Kate sniffed back her tears and pulled away. There were some wet spots on Nathan's jacket where she'd leaked all over him.

She tried to wipe it dry. "I'm sorry," she sniffed between sobs.

"What's going on," he pressed.

"He has her..." she explained.

"Who has who?"

"I... I don't know his name. He killed my aunt."

Nathan thought for a moment. "Fiona?"

"You read my file?"

"We're partners, of course, I did."

Kate nodded. It made perfect sense, after all, his life might depend on her one day. "Of course, you did."

"Your aunt's killer was never caught, though, right?"

"No, he wasn't but... Look, I have to tell you something. Something I did, years ago. I was just a kid. I was stupid."

"Weren't we all?"

Kate smiled. "I was always close to my aunt. We talked and texted, she told me everything. She told me about her boyfriend and the things he'd do to her. He hurt her, Nathan. Hit her. So when she died, I was convinced it was him. So I took matters into my own hands. I went and confronted him. I found him in the south of Ireland, near Cork. He attacked me, but I had an iron bar, so I hit him. It was self-defence, but he didn't get up."

"Did you kill him?" Nathan asked as he guided her to a seat and sat her down. He sat opposite and held her hands.

"No. He's alive, but he's brain-damaged. They never traced it to me."

"And he wasn't your aunt's killer." It was a statement, not a question.

"No, he wasn't. I'd visited the scene of Fiona's murder days before, and a man had talked to me while I was there. I didn't get a good look at him. Days later, I had a letter come through when I got back home. He admitted to killing her. He's been sending me letters ever since, taunting me, telling me he would show me what a real killer was like. Last night, he kidnapped my neighbour. He said he wanted this book, or he'd kill her."

"He's a part of the Black Hand, isn't he?"

Kate nodded. "I think so, yes."

"I thought so."

"You…" Kate blinked in shock. "You what?"

"I read up on your aunt's murder. I read about the sacrificial manner of her death. The symbols at the murder site. It all fits. But it was all circumstantial until today. I didn't want to link it until I knew for sure."

"Well, it's true. He's a part of the Black Hand, and he wanted this book. Said he'd provide a distraction for me…"

"I see," Nathan replied, glancing right. "Nice distraction."

"Did they kill anyone? If they killed anyone and I caused it…" Another sob burst forth and fresh tears stained her cheeks.

"I don't think so, but don't worry. It's not your fault. They did this."

"But, I put a man in a wheelchair! Left him brain-damaged for life."

"That is…"

"I'll resign," Kate blurted out. She wanted to beat him to it. She'd take this on the chin. She'd admit to it all and face the consequences.

"Don't be stupid," Nathan replied, bringing her up short.

"What?" Kate's breath caught.

"I said, don't be an idiot. You're not doing that. There's more to this than we know, so you're not going to admit to anything. How do you know Fiona's partner wasn't working for the Black Hand? Maybe you did the world a favour?"

"I mean, I guess. Maybe. But you know now. You know what I did."

"Yes, I do…"

"I can't ask you to keep that secret. That's not fair. I can't ask you…"

"Kate! Shut up for a moment."

Kate blinked, brought up short by Nathan's terse response.

"You told me a secret, so I'm going to tell you one, then we're even."

"I um, I didn't…"

"Just be quiet for one moment," Nathan said, raising a finger.

"Okay." She wasn't quite sure what was going on, but decided to go along with it for now.

"I've never told anyone this. If I had, I never would've gotten that promotion. In fact, I probably would've been put on leave or something to have my head looked at." Nathan took a breath. "When I was attacked, by this Dragon guy. I don't remember much, but one thing I do remember, very clearly, is looking up after being hit for the hundredth time and seeing a man drinking blood. I don't know what was going on, but I think the attack was interrupted. There were other people there that night, and they fought with the Dragon's gang. I don't remember much. I remember flashes of light. I remember feeling dizzy, and I remember looking up and seeing a man with blood all around his mouth, swallowing it down. I also remember his teeth. Oh God, his teeth," Nathan whispered, his eyes getting a distant, haunted look. "They weren't human."

"Shit," Kate whispered.

Nathan sighed. "Yeah. I thought I was going mad. I mean, I'd been hit in the head. I was delirious. I still don't know to this day if what I saw was real, or just mania or delusions brought on by the shock and pain I was in. Maybe it's both or neither. I don't know. But I've kept that all to myself. It probably wouldn't do much to me now. My reputation is well-known. But still, I kept it a secret, until today."

Kate was already feeling better. She'd calmed down as Nathan had told his story, and she'd realised that she probably wasn't the only one with secrets in this building. That didn't make her a bad person. Just human.

"Thank you for telling me," she said quietly.

Nathan nodded. "You're welcome."

Kate's eyes fell to the book at her feet. "So, what do we do now?"

"So, you said that this man, the one who killed your aunt, Fiona, he's a part of the Black Hand?"

"I mean, yeah. I think so. Makes sense, right?"

"Do you think he's the Dragon?"

Kate made a quiet gasp. "I don't know. I mean, maybe. That's possible."

"Either that, or maybe they're working together."

"I hadn't thought…"

Nathan looked down at the book, and then up at Kate. "I have an idea."

The door to the office opened, and Damon stuck his head through. "It's all over, no one was hurt," he said. "The boys in blue are out in their cars though. God knows if they'll find them. So, um, what's going on in here?"

Nathan looked back at Kate. He smiled and then at Damon again. "Do you trust us?"

Chapter 20

Kate turned the key, killing the engine. Sitting back in her seat, she took a deep breath, held it, and let it out slowly. She was on edge. This was a risky plan, but what other choice did she have?

An innocent life hung in the balance, and she didn't see any other way out of it. She had to play ball with this maniac.

There was nothing else for it.

If this worked, and she got Francine released, then, and only then, would she be able to breathe a little easier.

Kate concentrated on her breathing, taking another long, slow inhale through her nose, and then out through her mouth, doing her best to clear her mind, before finally picking up her phone and opening up the message thread. A little under half an hour ago, she'd replied to the killer.

'Got it, where do we make the exchange?'

It had taken only minutes before she got a short answer back.

'Millmead Car Park, by the River Wey in Guildford. 30 mins. Text when you arrive. I'll call you back.'

So here she sat, in a small car park consisting of two rows of cars facing each other just a few metres from the banks of the River Wey as it ran through Guildford's city centre.

The car park was maybe two-thirds full of cars and vans, and several people were either sitting watching the water flow by, feeding the ducks, or eating a late lunch. Shoppers walked through the area, crossing the bridge, walking out via the main road, or through one of the two pedestrian footpaths at the other end.

There were plenty of exits and lots of buildings overlooking the whole area. A pub stood nearby with a couple of patrons stood outside, smoking and laughing. Over the river, a large department store loomed, its rear windows watching the scene.

This place was thoroughly public in every way.

Kate looked around assessing the people that were milling about or sat in their cars.

Which ones were with Fiona's killer, or the Dragon, or both?

Nothing stood out as obvious, and Kate was not prepared to walk around accusing random people of being an accessory to murder.

Resigning herself to whatever happened, she returned her attention to her phone and tapped in a message.

'I'm here.'

She sent it and waited, feeling the tension in her shoulders build. The beginnings of a headache nagged at her temples.

Her phone rang.

Kate jumped, her heart suddenly hammering inside her ribcage. "Shit," she cursed and held up the device.

'Unknown number.'

"Of course." She took another beat to calm herself and answered the call.

"Hello?"

"You have it with you?" The voice was familiar and made her skin crawl.

"Of course. It's here, beside me."

"Well done. I knew you had it in you to do this. I knew from the moment you caved Duane's head in with barely a thought given to the consequences that you were my kind of girl. I like you, Kate."

"Can we get on with this?" Kate replied. She hated listening to his foul voice, it was like fingernails down a chalkboard.

"Now, now, Kate. This is a special moment, I don't want to rush it. You've taken your first steps down a new path. This is a big moment."

"If you say so."

"Kate, I suggest you be a bit more respectful if you want your neighbour back unharmed. I only need give the word, and I can have all kinds of things happen to her. Do you understand?"

Kate reined in her exasperation and clamped her mouth shut for a moment before speaking again. "Yeah, I understand."

"Good. Because if this goes well, I think we could have a nice little thing going on here. You know? A nice little back and forth. You help me, occasionally, and I don't destroy your life. I think that's being incredibly fair, don't you?"

"Totally," she answered, trying her best to sound sincere, and not like she wanted to be sick.

"Good."

"So, how do we do this?"

"Easy," he answered, "get out of the car and walk towards the bridge."

Kate pressed her lips together and took a long breath.

"Come on, don't get cold feet on me now," he urged her.

Kate climbed out and closed the door.

"There, you see? That was easy, wasn't it?"

He could see her.

He was somewhere close enough to see her. She didn't answer and started to slowly circle on the spot, scanning the waterfront, the car park, the pub, and all around, wondering if she could maybe spot him somewhere.

"Had a good look, have you?" he asked.

Kate grimaced. He was loving every moment of this.

"What do you want me to do?" She wasn't in the mood for his games, and just wanted Francine back.

"Walk towards the bridge, please. And Kate, taking the book with you."

Kate nodded. She walked round to the other side of her car and retrieved the bag containing the book from the passenger seat. Tucking it under her arm, she then crossed the car park, making for the footbridge that spanned the river.

"You see that brick post beside the bridge?" the killer asked.

Kate nodded. It was a squat, thick pillar of red brick, no taller than her waist, and was linked to a wall that was, in turn, connected to one side of the bridge.

"Yes."

"Put the book on there."

"Alright," she answered, and took a breath before asking her next question. "But, I want something from you first."

"Do you, Kate? Don't start getting ideas above your station, I won't stand for it."

"All I want is proof of life," Kate answered. "I want to see Francine. If I see her, then I'll leave the book, no questions asked."

There was silence on the end of the line for a moment. Kate waited, wondering if she'd pushed things too far. They had to demonstrate some good faith, though. This had to be a two-way exchange.

"You drive a hard bargain, Miss O'Connell, but I'll play your game. Look over the river, to the right."

Kate moved and stepped onto the bridge, keeping the book with her for the moment. She scanned the far bank and spotted Francine walking up along the side of the river with a young woman she recognised from Alister's security footage. The fake escort.

She stood beside Francine. In fact, it looked almost as if she were helping her walk or holding her up at least.

"If you've hurt her!" Kate warned.

"You'll do what?"

Kate bit her tongue and walked back to the pillar. "Okay, I'm putting the book down."

For a moment, she hesitated. She didn't like leaving the book here, but what choice did she have? It felt like their case against the Dragon and Fiona's killer was slipping away from them. She hoped it wasn't. She hoped that Nathan would pull something out of nowhere and save the day.

How he'd do it, was another question entirely, however.

Kate turned and crossed the bridge, walking quickly. Ahead, and to her right, around fifty metres away, the fake escort turned and left Francine where she was. Francine collapsed, her legs buckling beneath her.

"No." Kate immediately started sprinting. She charged off the end of the bridge and sprinted up the riverbank, the book forgotten as she raced over to Francine. She got to her side several seconds later, and dropped to a crouch beside her. She looked a little delirious.

Her face was strangely caked in makeup, for some reason. Kate wiped at it, revealing purple bruises beneath as Francine moaned in pain at her touch. They were hiding the damage they'd inflicted on her.

"Bastards," Kate cursed and grabbed her phone from her pocket. She tapped in 999.

"Which service do you require?"

"Ambulance please..."

Chapter 21

"How'd it go?" Nathan asked as they left Guildford behind, Nathan easing the car out into traffic on the A3 highway into Guildford.

Kate sighed. "They really hurt her," Kate answered, feeling like she'd failed Francine somehow by getting her mixed up in all this mess.

She knew the plan. She trusted Nathan, but here they were, with the book in the hands of Fiona's killer, and possibly the Dragon too, and yet they were still no closer to finding Alister's killer.

"I'm sorry," Nathan replied.

"It's okay. I just feel bad. I've really messed all this up. I've been an idiot. I should have come to you sooner."

"You didn't know how things would turn out," he reassured her. "I probably would have done the same. He's been taunting you for years. That can't have been easy."

Kate shook her head slowly. "No, it hasn't. Knowing he's out there, watching and waiting for his moment to strike. It's been a nightmare, frankly."

"I bet. So, did Francine tell you anything? Did she know where she'd been held?"

Kate shook her head. "No. She had no idea, and she's in no mood to talk, either. She was just getting upset by it, so I gave up. I didn't want to make things worse for her by making her relive it. It must have been terrifying."

Nathan nodded. "Doing that to an elderly woman is monstrous. The sooner we find him, the better. And speaking of which, I got permission to talk to Sandford's wife, Lisa. We'll head there now."

"Where is she?"

"Bookham."

"Oh, just up the road from us. Excellent," Kate replied, feeling her mood lighten. "Do you think she can help?"

"Sandford might hate me, but after it was proven beyond any reasonable doubt that he was a killer, Lisa ended up siding with me. She thanked me towards the end, for revealing who her husband really was. I think she thought she had a lucky escape."

"She probably did. If he can kill his lover, then he could have killed his wife."

"Those were her thoughts, too, I think."

"Okay, good. So at least we'll be welcomed by her, and not told to get lost."

"It'll make for a nice change, won't it?" Nathan replied, brightly.

"It'll certainly be a novelty."

"So, tell me about the drop, did it go well?"

Kate shrugged. "I don't know. I guess. He was certainly enjoying wrapping me around his finger."

"Hmm. Look, don't worry, we'll sort this. I think this was the only way."

Kate nodded. "I know. You're right. Thanks for your help."

"Anytime. It's what friends are for."

The ride up through Guildford and out the other side, heading East, took maybe twenty-five minutes. They passed Horsley Station on their way up the A25 and then the A246.

Kate gazed out the window at the brutalist building with the Surrey Police logo over the main entrance, and the scattering of bullet holes that now peppered the concrete facade. Several of the shattered windows were already boarded up. Predictably, the local and national press were already on site, reporting on the event.

"Looks like we're making news again," Kate remarked as they drove by.

"We seem to have a knack for doing that."

"Any update on it? Was anyone hurt?"

"There were a couple of non-fatal injuries, yeah. One was a bullet hit, the other was from shattered glass."

"Goddammit. I can't believe he did that. I hope this lead pans out." Kate felt terrible for agreeing to the killer's demands. It was such a stupid thing to do. Nathan had reassured her several times that she wasn't to blame and that there was little she could have done. A large part of her agreed, but she wasn't totally convinced.

If she'd just gone to Nathan earlier and told him about what Fiona's killer had been doing, maybe none of this would have happened and Francine wouldn't be in a hospital right now.

That was one of the worst parts. Seeing Francine lying on that bed, and seeing the pain and suffering that those thugs had caused her. They were scum. The worst of the worst, and she wouldn't rest until they were all locked up.

Nathan drove into the large village of Bookham and navigated to a street away from the high street. The houses were a mix of detached and semi-detached, mixed in with several bungalows. They were all set back from the road. Nathan pulled up outside a modest house and turned the engine off.

"Ready?" he asked.

Kate nodded and followed him up the walkway to the small front porch. The door was soon answered after a brief bell ring, and a blonde woman appeared at the door. She was slim and pretty. Kate understood why Sandford would go for her. Kate guessed he probably treated her as something like a trophy wife and wondered why he'd had flings with other girls when he had her at home.

"Nathan," Lisa said on opening the door. "It's lovely to see you. They said you'd be stopping by."

"I hope you don't mind the intrusion?"

"No, not at all. The kids are out with Dave, so I'm free for a bit. What can I do for you?" she asked as she led them inside.

"Can't you guess?"

Lisa looked back, her dusky eyes twinkled beneath her hair as she gave Nathan a resigned smile. "The usual, is it?"

"Bingo," Nathan replied. His jovial attitude made Kate smile. She didn't often see him like this with witnesses. She wondered if Nathan might be a little sweet on Lisa.

"Aren't you going to introduce me to your new partner?" Lisa asked.

"Sorry, yes, of course. This is DC Kate O'Connell."

"Nice to meet you, Kate. I love your hair."

"Thank you," Kate replied, blushing at the compliment.

"Sorry," Nathan said, looking back at her.

"That's okay," Kate replied.

"Dear me, Nate, you've not changed. Anyway, come in, sit down. I enjoy nothing better than discussing my ex-husband." Lisa pulled a face as she said it, which made Kate laugh. "So, what's he done this time?"

"Actually, I want to talk about some of the people that Sandford worked with, back before the murder. Did you know any of them?"

Lisa shrugged. "I met a handful, sure. But if you're talking about the shady stuff he used to do, and not the construction firm, then I'll be less useful to you. He kept that stuff very quiet, even from me. It only really came to light during your investigation."

Nathan nodded. "All the same, I'd like you to take a look at a photo for me and see if you recognise him."

"Sure. I'd like to help if I can."

Nathan pulled out the printout of the Dragon from the security footage and laid it on the coffee table before her.

Lisa took a long hard look, and a moment to think. "I'm sorry, no. I don't know who this is. Is this a new case?"

Nathan nodded. "It is, and we need to know who this man is. He's wanted for murder."

"I see. Well, I'm sorry, but I really don't know who that is. But now that I think of it, I do remember one man that Sandford hung around with and seemed to do some business with that I don't think was linked to the construction firm. It was Jon, someone... Jon... Oh, Parsons. That's it. Jon Parsons, yes. He was a businessman who worked in Croydon. He helped Sandford with his firm, but he was a bit of a shady character too. I didn't really like him, you know?" Lisa directed this last comment to Kate.

Kate nodded distractedly. That name rang a bell.

"Parsons?" Nathan asked.

"Yeah," Lisa replied. "Why?"

"I'm sure his name was in Sandford's file."

"It was," Kate agreed, suddenly remembering. "I remember seeing it. I think we have his details."

Nathan nodded. "We should be able to find him, then. So, you didn't like him?"

"No, and I could never really put my finger on it, you know? It was the way he looked at me and some of the little comments he made. He just gave me the creeps. Anyway, I've not seen him for ages, but I think you should follow up with him."

"Thank you, we will. That's a great help," Nathan replied.

"Anytime. You know that. I'm just sorry that it took you getting beaten up for the case to really come together."

"I'm alright now," Nathan reassured her.

"I know. Thanks for everything, though."

They said their farewells and returned to their car.

"Let's see what this Mr Parsons has to say for himself, shall we? Call it in and get an address."

Chapter 22

"Mr Parsons," Nathan said as he walked into the office on an industrial estate this side of Croydon. Kate followed him in, having gotten past his diligent secretary, and swept her eyes over the room. It was sparse and could frankly have done with a lick of paint and some TLC, but it was warm and comfortable. Two chairs sat on this side of Jon's desk, waiting for them.

Jon himself was a short man with thinning hair and a drawn look to his face. He was thin and wiry, with strong brows and a piercing gaze.

Nathan introduced them both.

"Hello," Jon replied. "Is there something I can help you with, officers?"

"We sincerely hope so," Nathan replied.

"Well, please, ask away. I'm always happy to help."

Kate frowned. He seemed a little keen for someone who was possibly involved in Sandford's more shady deals, even if that was a long time ago.

"Good. So, you used to work with Sandford Barret, right?"

Jon paused for a moment, as if considering Nathan's words, but Kate wondered if it was more to do with him wondering what she and Nathan actually knew about his operation. "Sandford?"

"That's right," Kate replied. You knew him, and you did business with him."

Jon took another moment to process that, looking between her and Nathan. "Um, yeah. That was a long time ago though, back before I found out he was a murdering son of a bitch."

"But you did work with him," Kate pressed.

Jon sighed. "Yes, I did."

"On what, exactly?"

"I don't know. That was a long time ago. My business has changed a lot since then, but we worked on a couple of projects together, yeah. There's nothing wrong with that."

"No," Nathan agreed. "No, there isn't, providing those projects weren't illegal."

"What are you here for?" Jon asked, his expression becoming stony.

"If you worked with Sandford, did you know some of the other people Sanford worked with?" Nathan asked.

"Anything I did back then is ancient history. I've not worked with Sandford or any of his cronies for years."

"So, you did work with some of the same people?"

"From time to time…" he answered with a sigh, clearly wanting this over with as soon as possible.

"What about this man?" Nathan asked, placing the image of Alister's killer on the table. "The Dragon."

"Aww, shit," Jon replied, as all the colour drained from his face. He seemed to physically recoil from the image as if the very thought of it offended him.

"I'd say that's a big fat yes," Kate answered with a smile.

"What are you doing dragging all this up?" Jon asked. "I've been out of this for ages. I want nothing more to do with it. Do you hear me? Nothing. These people are nothing but trouble."

"You know them well, then?" Nathan answered.

"Did you not hear me? These are dangerous people," he reiterated. "You do *not* want to mess with them."

"Oh, we know," Nathan replied. "Don't we?"

"Absolutely," Kate agreed. "We know exactly what kind of person he is."

Jon's eyes flicked between them. "What are you not telling me. What has he done?"

"He's the subject of a murder investigation. We know he did it, we just need to find him, because surprisingly, there's no one in the phone book called The Dragon."

"Yeah, funny that," Kate replied. "They need to list gang names in there really."

"A missed opportunity if ever there was one. So, you clearly know who this Dragon guy is," Nathan said, returning his attention to Jon. "Care to share that information with us?"

"I'm not getting involved. No way."

"We thought you might say that, didn't we?" Kate remarked. There was no way she was letting him wriggle out of this one. She felt like they were close. He knew something, she was sure of it.

Nathan nodded to her. "Indeed, it was always a distinct possibility."

Kate nodded. "So, we did some digging on you, and our team found some interesting things. Not least of which, were some of the deals with Sandford himself."

"You were a slippery little weasel, weren't you Jon," Nathan commented.

"You've got nothing on me," Jon protested.

"Maybe, maybe not, but we do have a lot of evidence that would get you back into court and tie you up for a while," Nathan threatened him. "You always seemed to get out on some kind of technicality, and never see any jail time. But the testimony by Beth Carlisle, one of the models from the Bellrose Agency was very compelling. I wonder if she's changed her mind about going on the record about that yet?"

"I'm sure I could have a chat with her about that," Kate mused. "Woman to woman. You know."

"And then there's Nic Lacey," Nathan suggested.

"Oh yes," Kate agreed. "His story about what you did to him and his business back when you were working with Sandford..."

"Alright!"

"You might wriggle out of these one more time for all we know, but what would that do to your livelihood, and your business? Would you survive?" Nathan asked.

"Does your current partner know about this?" Kate asked.

"You could have another one of those woman-to-woman chats," Nathan suggested.

"Oh yes, I'd love to," Kate replied brightly. "I'm sure she'd love to hear these stories."

"I said alright," Jon spoke up. "I'll help you. What do you want to know?"

Nathan prodded his finger at the dog-eared printout. "Who is that?"

Jon sighed and seemed to collapse into his chair. "So, there's nothing else I can help you with? It has to be this?"

Nathan nodded as Kate sat on the edge of her seat. Would this be the key piece of information? Would this finally lead them to the killer? To Fiona's killer? She just needed to give him one final push.

"I think we have your partner's phone number..." Kate said, pulling out her mobile, hoping this would be enough.

"If he finds out I spoke to you, he'll kill me," Jon stated. "You know that, right?"

"He's already killed, we won't let him do it again," Nathan replied.

"He's crazy," Jon replied. "Thinks he's got some kind of dragon spirit inside him or something. He's legit insane."

"Do you want us to show you what he did to an old man?" Kate pressed.

"Okay, fine. I'll tell you his name, but I can't get involved. He must never know this came from me."

Kate looked over at Nathan, she wasn't sure how to answer that one.

"We'll see what we can do," Nathan replied.

Jon screwed up his face. He didn't look convinced, but she knew they had him between a rock and a hard place. They could mess up his life easily enough, if they needed to. Kate didn't like the idea of strong-arming him, but they needed this. They needed his name.

"Alright, fine. His name is Terry Sims. Okay? There, I told you. God help me."

"Terry Sims?" Nathan asked.

Jon nodded. "He's a psycho, man. A freaking psycho."

"And where do we find Terry?"

"Hold on, I've got his address somewhere," he replied as he began to riffle through an address book. "He has a place in

Sutton, on an industrial estate. Some kind of gym or boxing place. I've been there a few times, back in the day. But he'll be there, as usual. Aaah, here it is." He showed them the address.

Kate took a photo of it on her phone. "Thanks."

"Are you going over there?"

Nathan smiled. "That's kind of what we do."

"Take back up," Jon warned. "They'll be armed, and they won't hesitate to shoot."

"You're sure of that?"

Jon nodded. "He once showed me the small arsenal of guns he has there and bragged how he'd kill any pigs that turned up. I don't think he was kidding."

Chapter 23

Kate followed Nathan into the main office of Horsley Station and knew right away that something was up. DI Mason and DS Taylor were stood nearby, talking between themselves.

"I guess you don't think we can handle our own shit, right?" Sam Mason said as they stepped in. The comment was directed at Nathan.

"What?" Nathan asked.

"Nah, it's not that. He just likes the eye candy. Can't blame him, though," DS Taylor added. "I'd like a sexy spy woman on my team."

"What are you talking about?" Kate asked.

"Boss?" a voice said before they could answer.

Kate and Nathan both turned.

"Zafar, what's up?" Nathan asked.

"We did as you asked when you called in and got in touch with Damon," he began, as they fell into step beside Zafar. "We told him about Terry Sims, the Dragon, but he said he couldn't get away, so he sent someone over to go with you on the raid."

"Oh?" Kate asked. "Who?"

"A woman. She has a Government ID which checks out, and she seems familiar with the case. Malcolm's in there with her now, but I just thought you should know."

"What's her name?"

"Rebecca Chance."

"Oh," Kate answered, remembering her from their first meeting with Damon in the Chief's office.

"So what's Damon doing now?" Nathan asked.

"No idea, he wouldn't elaborate other than to say he was following up a lead."

Nathan nodded. Kate wondered if this had to do with their case and the book they'd given away, or if this was something new.

"Alright, where's Rebecca?"

"Incident Room," Zafar replied and walked across with them.

Kate followed Nathan inside. Sure enough, the dark-haired woman stood in the middle of the Incident Room, casually chatting with DCI Dean.

"Aaah, here they are," the DCI said. "I didn't know you were involving the foreign office in this."

Rebecca smiled.

"That was Damon's call," Kate answered, improvising. She had no idea what Damon was doing sending Rebecca here to help with the raid, but she had a feeling she was about to find out. "They're throwing everything at this."

"Hey. Good to see you again," Rebecca said. "I'll be under your command on the raid. Just to be clear. This is your gig."

"Thank you," Nathan replied.

"I've got an armed response team ready to go," Rachel said as she walked over. "They're downstairs."

"Great, thanks. So what do we have on the gym?" Nathan asked her.

"Not loads, unfortunately," Rachel replied.

"Whatever we do have, we printed off and put up here," Zafar added, nodding to the big board. "It looks like an upstairs gym, and we can get a basic idea of layout from the photos on its crappy website. From what we can tell, it's got two entrances, the main one out front and a fire escape at the back."

Nathan nodded. "Standard pincer movement, then," he suggested. "Go in both entrances and trap them inside."

"Sounds like a plan, boss," Zafar answered.

Nathan stood up straight and looked at Kate. "What do you think?"

"Don't look at me, I'm not the tactical genius," She answered. "But sure, sounds good."

"I'll be going in with you two," Rebecca remarked.

Kate nodded; she hoped Rebecca wouldn't get in the way.

***

Kate sat in the back of the armed police van, right up against the cab. Nathan on her right, while Rebecca sat opposite her, looking bored.

She'd been through several stressful situations during her time as an officer, but this was her first time as part of an armed response unit, going in hard and fast.

As the van bumped and juddered over the roads, she couldn't quite keep still and kept tapping her knee or fiddling with things. She pulled her gun out to check it over for the umpteenth time.

"You've checked it once, right?"

Kate looked at Rebecca, who'd leant forward to speak to her.

"Um, yeah," she answered. She'd checked it way more than once.

"Then put it away and leave it alone."

Kate glanced down at her gun and back up at Rebecca before nodding, and holstering her weapon.

Rebecca had changed her black jeans and top to a more layered, but still black, outfit with straps and pouches for her weapons and ammunition. She held a sleek, suppressed sub-machine gun loosely in her lap, as if it were nothing. Kate didn't recognise the make of the weapon. As Rebecca sat back and smiled, she looked utterly calm and relaxed. But that just made Kate feel even more nervous.

How could she be so chill in a situation like this?

"One minute," one of the armed officers called out.

"Are you ready for this?" Nathan asked her, placing his hand on her arm.

Kate nodded. "Of course, I'll be fine." She didn't feel fine. She wanted to throw up right there in the back of the van. But she daren't admit it.

Not in front of stone-cold Rebecca Chance.

She busied herself with her final preparations, including popping a pair of earplugs in, just in case things got noisy. Who was she kidding? Of course, they were going to get noisy.

That last minute seemed to drag on forever until the van came to a screeching halt and the back doors were flung open. The armed officers deployed in quick, practised movements, setting up a perimeter, while an advance team made for the main doors of the building. Rebecca was up before both of them. She moved to the end of the van, before looking back at them.

"Stay behind me."

Kate nodded as she pulled out her gun. She wasn't about to argue with that.

Craning her neck, she watched as the team burst in through the front doors without a moment's hesitation, and moved inside. She knew there was a second-team in another van going in through the back.

Rebecca waited several moments and then jumped to the ground.

"Let's go," she said. Kate followed, but they were barely two metre from the van when the first gunshots rang out. Rebecca ducked but kept moving. Kate crouched too, but paused. When she saw Rebecca keep going, she silently cursed herself and hustled to keep up.

Stupid. She shouldn't have stopped moving.

Rebecca moved to the side of the main door and waited for Kate and Nathan to form up beside her. Kate had barely made it before Rebecca stepped out with her gun up and at her shoulder. She approached the door, checking her corners and moving like she'd done this a thousand times before.

"Let's go," Rebecca said and moved inside.

It felt like she was their personal bodyguard. She smiled at the thought. She could get used to this.

With her gun raised, Kate walked into the building beside Nathan. There was an officer guarding the door to an unrelated business while more officers inside were ushering the innocent workers out.

Rebecca made her way up the stairs. Kate followed, noting the large boxing tournament posters that hung on the walls. Ahead, more gunfire sounded, reverberating through the building. Even with her earplugs in, it was mind-numbingly noisy.

At the top, Rebecca led them through a doorway. To their right, an intense firefight was going on between the police and several armed men who had dug themselves in at the back of the main room.

Their forces were almost entirely focused on that battle.

"Hey," Kate shouted at the nearest officer and pointed up the corridor, away from the fighting. "Anyone go this way?"

"Two guys," the officer replied. "Don't know where they are now."

Kate glanced at Nathan. He nodded.

"Let's check it out," he said.

Rebecca took point as they moved up the corridor, their guns up and ready.

They crept slowly, approaching the first door cautiously. Rebecca cleared it, checking inside, and moved past, making for the second one. She was seconds away from it when a man stepped out with a gun in hand.

Kate went to adjust her aim, but Rebecca moved much quicker than she did and calmly fired off two shots, dropping him cleanly, only for another man to step out of another door to her left holding a machete.

The thug swung the huge blade at Rebecca, who reacted with grace and ease. Blocking the swing with her off-hand, she let go of her weapon. It swung from its strap while she slammed the heel of her palm into the man's face.

Kate watched as a third man rushed Rebecca, but at no time did Kate think she was in any way overwhelmed.

Movement on her right pulled her attention away from Rebecca's well-honed movements. A man ran towards them from the first room. She'd missed his approach and cursed. He threw a glass bottle at Nathan that knocked him on his ass. Kate ducked back. He rushed her, holding a freaking sword in his off-hand!

What the hell?!

Moving left, she dodged his initial swung and brought her gun to bear, shoving it into the man's gut. She fired once.

A look of shock filled his face as he staggered back and fell against the wall. The attacker dropped his blade and clutched his stomach, gritting his teeth in agony.

Looking up, Rebecca stood tall above three thoroughly beaten men and looked back. Kate could only gape at the sight, unable to believe what she was seeing.

"You okay?" Rebecca asked.

"Yeah, fine," Kate answered.

"Never better," Nathan agreed as he took his time getting up.

"Let's check the last few rooms," Rebecca urged.

Back on her feet, Kate helped Nathan up and brushed herself down. "Sure, why not."

Moving through the next few back rooms, Rebecca approached the final doorway. She raised her hand to signal that they should hold their ground. Kate froze as Rebecca inched ahead.

Someone yelled off to her right. Kate turned to see the female gang member break cover. She raised a gun and fired.

Kate ducked, dropping to her left. The thug's shots went wide. Kate took half a breath to steady her nerves and aimed as carefully as she could in that split second. She squeezed the trigger. Her instructor would be proud.

Kate's gun barked.

Blood splattered out of the woman's thigh as she dropped to the floor with a scream.

Holding still, Kate wondered if there would be any more surprises, but the building had finally fallen silent. Even the gun battle in the main gym room had stopped.

"Well done, good shooting," Rebecca complimented her.

"Thanks," she replied as she did her best to catch her breath.

"You both okay?"

"Peachy," Nathan replied.

"Ditto," Kate agreed. "Who's in there?"

"Our two missing officers. Come on, they could do with our help."

Getting up, Kate watched Nathan cuff the woman she'd shot before moving back to check that the gun battle had gone in their favour. Kate moved into the last room, where she found the two men. Both were badly injured from gunshot flesh wounds and a severe beating, but Kate hoped they'd live.

Moving back into the previous room, Kate wandered over to the woman whose leg was bleeding profusely. Looking around, she spotted a length of rag and quickly wrapped it around the woman's leg. Pulling it tight to stem the bleeding, Kate got her to lay back awkwardly, her cuffed hands behind her back, and raise her leg up.

"Impersonate escorts often, do you?" Kate asked.

The woman was puffing and panting against the pain. "Fuck off."

"Where's Terry?"

"Not here," she blustered.

"Smart arse," Kate replied. "I guessed that. So where is he?"

"Dunno'," she answered, clearly not keen on answering any questions.

"He fled," Rebecca called out from the other room with the injured officers. "These guys saw him outside, getting into a car."

The woman beside her smirked.

"Shit," Kate hissed.

Nathan walked back into the room. "The building's secure. Any sign of Terry Sims?"

"He got out," Kate answered.

"Damn it." Nathan's phone rang. He fished it out of his pocket and glanced at the screen. "It's Damon."

"I hope it's good news," Kate replied as Nathan took the call.

Chapter 24

The car bumped up the dirt track. Stones popped beneath the tyres as it continued up the slope. Ahead, trees closed in as night began to fall.

"You're sure this is right?" Kate asked, frowning at the landscape.

"This is where Damon said to meet him," Nathan answered.

"Keep going," Rebecca stated from the back seat. "He'll be further up."

Kate saw Nathan shrug beside her, before urging the car onwards in the deepening night. A few hundred metres ahead, around a corner and well into the wooded area, Kate spotted a car parked off to the side of the road, with two people standing beside it. She recognised both. It was Damon and the redheaded woman who'd been at the first meeting she and Nathan had with him.

She couldn't remember her name, though. She looked scruffy dressed in ripped jeans and a tank top.

"What's she doing here?" Kate said.

"Dunno," Nathan answered. Rebecca stayed silent.

Nathan pulled up behind Damon's car and Kate stepped out. Damon approached with a smile.

"Glad you could make it," he said and offered his hand in greeting. They each shook it.

"Any luck?" Nathan asked.

Damon's grin only grew wider. "Oh, ye of little faith. Of course. The book's in a house, just over that way."

Kate looked to her left and into the trees over the road.

"Through there?"

"There's a large estate on the other side of those trees, you passed the entrance to it about a hundred metres back."

Kate felt some of the tension in her shoulders fade as she sighed in relief. "So, it worked then?"

"Perfectly," Damon replied. "He never knew I was there."

"That's a relief. So, now we just need to get it back."

"Indeed," Damon replied with a smile, adjusting his glasses. "We'll head there now."

"Now?" Nathan asked. "Are we authorised to do that?"

"We are. Besides. You'd be pursuing a suspect."

Kate cocked her eyebrow at him. "How so?"

"Terry's in there. He got there a little while before you did."

"You know that for sure? And that the book's in there?"

Damon glanced at the redhead and then back. "One hundred percent."

Kate looked over at Nathan and shrugged. "Sounds good. What do you think?"

"Yeah. Should we call it in?" Nathan asked.

"No, not yet," Damon replied. "We are stretching the rules a little here, but you're working under my auspice on this, so I'll deal with it. You remember Amanda, by the way?" He gestured towards the redhead.

Kate nodded at the woman who stood slightly behind Damon, watching the conversation. She looked calm and relaxed with her hands in her back pockets.

"What's the craic?" Amanda asked, a soft Irish accent colouring her words.

"Hi," Kate answered.

"Hello," Nathan greeted her.

"Does she work with you?" Kate asked Damon. It was a little rude with Amanda right there, but Kate wasn't in the mood to mess about.

Damon gave Amanda a side-eye. "In a way. Trust me, she'll be helpful. We need her."

Amanda grinned. "Nice to know I'm useful."

"Yeah, sure, why not," Kate answered, letting some exasperation seep through into her words.

"Gear up," Damon urged. "This could be dangerous."

Rebecca approached Damon's car while Kate moved with Nathan to the back of his, where he popped the trunk. The car's boot opened wide, revealing a selection of equipment, including an armoured vest for each of them.

"What do you think of all this?" Kate whispered to Nathan.

"It's highly unusual," Nathan remarked. "We should be calling in for back up, not heading in there like some kind of action heroes."

Kate nodded. "True. But I feel better knowing Rebecca is here. Did you see her at the gym?"

Nathan nodded. "She's a capable girl."

"You're not kidding. She kicks ass."

Kate finished securing her armoured vest and checked her gun. She'd already fully reloaded it after the raid in Sutton. Satisfied, she stepped back around to where Damon and the two women stood waiting. They were an odd-looking trio, Kate thought. Rebecca looked like some kind of special forces agent in her fitted black outfit. Damon wore an armoured vest over his shirt with the word 'POLICE' emblazoned across it, similar to Nathan and herself. But Amanda was carrying no weapons and didn't wear any armour.

"Do you need a spare vest?" Kate asked, her eyes flicking between Amanda and Damon.

"Thank ye, no. I'll be grand," Amanda replied.

Kate sighed at the absurdity of it all. "Okay, if you're sure." She glanced at Nathan, who looked just as bewildered as she felt.

"We should get in there, so we should," Amanda commented.

"Indeed," Damon replied. "Let's get going." Rebecca took the lead and took off at a jog. Kate made to follow but noticed that Damon walked at a more sedate pace. "Shouldn't we... Uh, oh? Where's Amanda gone?"

The woman had completely disappeared. There was no sign of her anywhere, despite her having been there just seconds before.

Damon looked round and returned his attention to Kate with a shrug. "I don't know. She'll be around."

"Around?" Nathan asked.

"What? Like, where?" Kate added.

Damon shrugged and set off with Nathan at his heels. "I don't know. Now, come on."

Pausing at the edge of the woods, Kate looked about, but there was no sign of her.

"What the hell?" she whispered, before turning and setting off after Damon. She caught them a moment later, but Rebecca had ranged well ahead and was out of sight.

"Your methods are a little unorthodox," Kate said as she fell into step beside the two men.

"I know. I understand your confusion. But it's the nature of the work that I do on behalf of the NCA. You'll understand as you do more with us, but we have a wide latitude to do what we need to when it comes to dealing with these kinds of events. As you know, they're not typical, and some of them can get…well, a little weird, so we use a lot of outside resources."

"Like Rebecca and Amanda?" Nathan asked.

"Exactly," Damon replied. "They're not part of the NCA, but have links to organisations that have similar goals and work with us on occasion. We don't use those resources often, but sometimes they're very useful."

"She'd need to be, without any weapons or armour, and what's with the relaxed dress code with her?"

"Look, I don't know everything, I just get told to work with certain people, and from what I've seen, Amanda can handle herself perfectly well. It's not something I get to ask questions about and expect to get any answers on."

"I understand," Kate said. "Look."

Between the trees, a tall metal fence blocked their way, but part of it had been cut and bent back, leaving enough space for them to squeeze through. Kate went first and kept watch while the other two followed. The trees on this side were spaced further apart and stretched off up the gentle hill.

"I take it that's where we're headed?" Nathan asked.

Kate followed his gaze and spotted the faint glow of lights peeking through the undergrowth.

"That's the house," Damon confirmed. "Come on."

Setting off, they picked their way through the shadows as night took hold, leaving only the moon to light their way through the trees. Ahead, Kate spotted an unusual lump on the grass that she thought looked suspicious, and with a short whistle, pointed it out to the other two.

With their guns up and ready, they approached. As she edged around it, Kate realised it was a prone figure, lying at an unnatural angle.

"I'm going to have a look," Kate said.

Nathan nodded, keeping his gun up as he scanned the area.

Sneaking over, Kate soon spotted the man's security vest. She thought he was a police officer at first, but on second glance, she quickly realised it was just an unconscious security guard. She could see a cut on his brow and some slowly forming bruises.

"Clear," she hissed. The guys soon joined her. "Rebecca?"

"Looks like her handiwork," Nathan agreed.

"They really should invest in better security," Damon said. "Holes in their fence and narcoleptic security guards. It's not good."

Kate smiled.

"Come on, let's keep going," Damon suggested and struck out into the night once more. Kate fell into step beside him as they made for the house that was slowly coming into view up ahead. It was huge, judging by the lights. A sprawling mansion hidden away in the Surrey countryside.

A long minute later, they reached the edge of the treeline. Ahead, a wide-open space separated them from more bushes and trees closer to the house, which stood out clearly against the starry sky beyond.

"We'll jog," Damon suggested. "I don't want to be out in the open too long."

Kate nodded.

"You're okay to run, right?" Damon asked Nathan.

"Hey, I'm not that old."

"You should've brought your walking frame, grandpa," Kate said with a smile.

Nathan rolled his eyes. "Walking frame? Nah, I want one of them ride-on buggy things. That way, I can terrorise people."

"You so would," Kate agreed.

"Come on, then," Damon urged, ignoring their back and forth. He set off across the lawn.

Kate followed, keeping her gun pointed safely towards the ground, and hustled across the grass. She reached the other side without incident, and Nathan joined them, bringing up the rear.

"Nice of you to join us, slowcoach," Kate remarked.

"Piss off."

"Another sleepy guard over here," Damon notified them.

Kate looked and sure enough, another man in a guard's uniform lay unconscious in the grass, most likely knocked out by Rebecca.

"Remind me never to get on Rebecca's bad side," Nathan commented.

"Some men pay good money to be abused like this," Kate remarked.

"Some men are freaks," Nathan answered as they moved past the body, and closer to the house. As they walked, Kate spotted movement up ahead. A second later, Rebecca appeared from between two bushes, followed by Amanda.

Kate blinked. *How did she get here so quickly?*

"Keep heading that way," Amanda said, pointing towards the rear of the house. "Make for the formal garden at the back."

Damon nodded. "Will do."

Amanda smiled, leaving Kate a little a little bewildered. She understood that this woman was from some organisation with stupidly high clearance, but still, it was odd. Plus, she was like some kind of ninja, disappearing every time Kate looked away.

"Come on," Damon urged. Kate followed beside Nathan and gave him a look. Nathan bugged his eyes for a second before refocusing on the way ahead. Kate looked back, but Amanda had disappeared again.

She spotted Rebecca, though, who was now ranging off to their right and quickly disappeared into the foliage.

"What the hell?" Kate remarked.

"What's up?" Nathan asked.

"Amanda, she just disappeared again, like she wasn't even there."

"She does that," Damon answered. "Can take a little getting used to."

"The girl's like Batman," Kate remarked.

"You mean Batgirl," Nathan suggested.

"Whatever," Kate replied.

"What on earth?" Nathan gasped several seconds later.

Kate looked up to see flashes of light coming from up ahead, lighting up the leaves and branches around them. She heard a series of pops and bangs, followed by confused shouting. The lights inside the house suddenly died.

"Holy crap, what's going on?" Kate said.

People screamed amidst the snaps and explosions while light flashed again.

"Let's go," Damon said and jogged ahead. Kate followed Damon through several bushes and around a couple of trees, their twigs catching Kate on the face as she moved. She burst out of the undergrowth behind Damon onto a path. To her right, an archway cut into a well-maintained hedgerow beckoned them on.

Several people of varying ages suddenly ran through the arch, looking panicked. They saw Kate and the others, and gave them a wide birth.

"In there, please," a woman in long, strange robes said.

Damon made for the arch. "Come on."

Kate followed with Nathan on her heels, unsure what exactly was going on. Through the arch, it opened up into a large, flat, open space surrounded by the hedge. To Kate's left, the rear of the vast house rose, reaching for the stars, while on her right, the formal garden spread out before them. A long, central pond stretched up the middle, surrounded by geometric pathways that were boarded with flowerbeds. Several groupings of people ran through the area, heading in all directions. It was chaos. All of them wore strange red and black robes.

"What the pissing hell is all this?"

"Come on," Damon urged, and they moved up the side of the garden, towards the largest concentration of people, but they were dispersing quickly. "Whatever they were doing, it looks like we arrived before things got out of hand."

"What do you mean?" Kate asked, feeling confused.

"Oh, crap. They were enacting a ritual, weren't they?" Nathan stated.

"That's right," Damon replied. "I'm guessing the book will be this way. Come on."

They jogged up the garden as a group, ducking and dodging around fleeing people.

"Look, there," Nathan said, pointing ahead. Kate followed his gesture and spotted a shirtless Terry Sims further up the garden at the far end of the pond. "That's him. That's Alister's killer."

"It is," Kate agreed, thrilled that they were finally closing in on their target. He was stood just behind a woman in glittering green robes with long dark hair. Nearby, Kate spotted Amanda marching towards the woman in green.

What is she doing?

Nathan slipped through the next group of people, taking the lead.

"Hey, Terry," he shouted and charged ahead.

"Nathan, no," Kate called after him, but her voice was muffled by the scrum of people that pushed past her. "Goddammit," she hissed. "Police, move!"

"Oi!" A man stepped out in front of them with a gun in one hand, and an extended baton in the other. "You're trespassing," he shouted, focusing on Damon.

Kate aimed her gun as she emerged from between two people to get a better shot. "Don't," she warned him. "This is police business."

The guard looked up, spotted her, and adjusted his aim, bringing his gun to bear.

Kate grunted her frustration and fired her gun for the second time today, aiming at his centre mass. Her aim was true, and the man was knocked off his feet. He stumbled and fell, gasping for breath. Kate ran up and couched beside him. A quick check confirmed she'd hit his armoured vest.

"I'll deal with him," Damon barked at her. "Go get Nathan."

Kate heard another gunshot.

She looked up to see Nathan grappling with Terry who was roaring at him. Blood welled up from Terry's leg where Nathan had shot him. Nathan held Terry's right arm with his left, doing his best to keep the dagger Terry held at a distance.

Terry was a big man, and as Kate approached, her gun raised, he forced Nathan down.

"Shit," Kate cursed, seeing where this was going, but she didn't have a clear shot. She ran. She glanced up looking for Amanda and the woman in green, but they were nowhere to be seen.

"No, arrgh," Nathan grunted as the dagger descended.

"Oh yes," Terry shouted. "You'll make a worthy sacrifice."

Kate charged at Terry. Holding her gun with two hands, she swung it at the back of his head. The metal of the handle smashed into his skull. He dropped, rolling away with a cry of pain.

He rolled onto his back, one hand holding his head as Kate stood over him, pointing her gun at his bare chest, and the intricate dragon tattoo that covered it.

"It's over Terry."

The large man smiled as Nathan rolled away beside her with a groan. "It's never over, Kate."

"It's over for you."

"Our work will continue, it always will."

"You're under arrest for the murder of Alister Langley. You do not have to say anything. But it may harm your defence if you do not mention when questioned something which you later rely on in court. Anything you do say may be given in evidence. Do you understand?"

Terry smirked. "Whatever."

"Where's your boss?"

Terry frowned. "My boss?"

"The man who coordinated the switch of the book and Francine?"

Terry laughed. "He's not my boss."

"What's his name, Terry?"

"Why do you want to know?"

"Indulge me," Kate remarked. She spotted Damon out of the corner of her eye, helping Nathan.

"Give me one reason why I should."

Kate shrugged. "Maybe I'll go easy on you?"

Terry laughed.

"Tell me!" Kate bellowed, feeling her anger and emotions rise. She was so close to finding out who the hell her aunt's killer was. If she could only get a name.

"Alright, sure. I'll play," Terry replied.

Kate's breath caught. Was he really going to tell her?

"His name's Abban Devlin," Terry pronounced.

Kate blinked, unable to quite believe that he'd told her his name. "Abban," she repeated, her mind racing as she thought about what it meant to know who had been taunting her. Maybe she'd be able to find him, and end this nightmare.

"That's him."

Kate frowned and focused her attention back on the man lying at her feet. "Where is he? Where is Abban?"

Terry smiled. "Right behind you."

Kate felt something hard and cold prod the side of her head, followed by the distinct sound of the hammer of a gun being cocked.

Kate slid her eyes to her left and twisted her head slightly, bringing the gun and the man holding it into view. He smiled, and shock washed over her as she stared at a man she recognised.

"Clyde?" Kate gasped. It was her neighbour.

"Abban, actually Kate. But you can call me Clyde if you like."

"Fucker," Kate hissed. He'd been living next door to her for months.

"The gun," Abban ordered. Kate glanced around. Damon was holding onto Nathan, who looked hurt from his fight with Terry and was in no shape to help. Beneath her, Terry smiled and started to sit up.

Unable to see a way out of it, and not feeling at all confident that she could grab and disarm Abban, she slowly raised her hands.

"Alright, you win," she said.

ZA-SPANG!

Abban screamed.

Glancing left, Kate saw Abban's gun hit the ground with a metallic thud. He held his hand up as he cried out. Blood flowed from his ruined fingers.

Terry shifted below her. She kicked out and smashed her boot into his face, putting him face down in the mud. She looked up to see Rebecca perhaps a hundred metres away, relaxing her weapon. Rebecca nodded to her once. Kate nodded back. Beyond Rebecca, a helicopter rose up and flew away. Rebecca stepped out of view.

She'd shot Abban's gun out of his hand, right beside her head.

She didn't have time to appreciate the skill it took to do that as she turned to see Abban already sprinting away towards the darkened house, as fast as he could go.

"Go get him," Nathan shouted as he and Damon fell onto Terry and cuffed him while he lay unconscious.

Kate nodded. She turned and charged after Abban as he ran for the house. He had a good lead on her and charged out of sight through another arch in the hedge. Kate pushed herself harder and ran out of the formal garden, spotting a back door that was moving slightly. Kate ran for it and bumped up against the wall where she stopped. She caught her breath and raised her gun before moving inside. Checking her corners, she stepped into the large, dark wooden-floored room. In the murky depths of the room, it was difficult to make out much in the way of detail. There was hardly any furniture, but there were plenty of doors that led deeper into the house.

She turned in a slow circle, looking all around. It was quiet. Most of the terrified people outside had gone, and the building itself was silent.

The sound of her laboured breathing and the thumping of her heart filled her ears instead.

"I know you're in here, Abban," she called out.

"What are you going to do, Kate? Arrest me?" his voice echoed through the room, making it difficult to pinpoint.

"The thought had crossed my mind," she answered as she peered into the darkness. The darkness was all-consuming and the statues set into the walls were confusing.

"Do you think that's wise, Miss O'Connell? With what I know?"

"Why, what do you know?" She needed him to keep talking.

"Don't be cute with me," Abban replied. "You know well enough what I know. I can ruin you, and you know it."

"You know, I'm not sure I do."

"You don't think I'll do it?"

"And expose yourself?" Kate asked.

"I'll take you down with me. Besides, good luck proving I killed Fiona. You have no proof. Instead, the media storm will end your career before it's really even begun."

Kate felt sure the voice was coming from the right side of the room, and moved that way, approaching a door through to another shadowy space.

"Now, you see, I don't think it will. I've already told Nathan and Damon what happened. And Damon has assured me that they will protect me from any repercussions. Besides, I think an investigation into Duane's past will reveal more about you and the Black Hand than it will about me."

Abban didn't reply.

"What's up, cat got your tongue?" she asked, mimicking his earlier taunt.

"Arrrrgh!" Footsteps hammered across the wooden floor. Kate turned to see Abban charging at her from the shadows holding a metal statue.

A confident, calm stillness washed over her as she brought her gun to bear on the charging man. He held the improvised weapon high with his mouth wide. Fury etched across his face.

Kate aimed and fired.

Abban spun and dropped to the floor, the statue sliding away over the polished floorboards. He writhed in pain as he held his shoulder with his ruined hand. He was missing a couple of fingers and leaking blood everywhere. Kate holstered her gun and grabbed him, turning him onto his stomach before slapping a pair of cuffs on him.

With Abban secure, she stepped back and sat down on the wooden floor. She sighed as she sat there looking at him. He turned to face her and grimaced in pain.

"How did you find me?"

Kate smiled. "You know, for a moment, you nearly had me," Kate admitted. "I tried to do as you wanted. I tried to get the book out of the station, but Nathan caught me, so I told him everything. Then Damon turned up. That's when we came up with the plan. The NCA traced your call to me during the drop-off. From there, they could just follow you here. So that was your mistake. You thought I wouldn't tell anyone, that I couldn't trust anyone. Turns out, that's exactly what I needed to do."

"Bitch," Abban muttered turning his head away and hissing with pain.

Kate grunted and lay back on the floor. She was shattered, and for the first time in a long time, the weight that came with Abban's Sword of Damocles was gone. For the first time in a long, long time she felt free.

She couldn't help but laugh. "I never thought I'd be happy to be called a bitch, but there it is."

Chapter 25

"I hear congratulations are in order," Chief Superintendent Collins said as he stood behind his desk smiling at Kate, Nathan, Damon, and DCI Dean as they entered.

Kate smiled back.

"Thank you, sir," Nathan replied.

"Seriously, that's good work. Two major arrests in one go. You all did well."

"We lost the book they wanted to steal from Alister though," Kate admitted. They had no idea where it had gone and presumed it had been taken by one of the fleeing attendees at the gathering they'd disrupted.

Kate felt bad for having given it to Abban, but that loss was almost entirely offset, knowing that he was finally behind bars, for now at least.

"A small price to pay," the Chief answered. "The main thing is that you got your man."

"We did, sir. Terry Sims is in custody and is unlikely to be given bail, given the severity of his crimes."

The Chief nodded. "And this Abban? Strange name."

"We have him, too. His future is less certain. If we can't pin Fiona Dunn's murder on him, then he won't be locked up for long."

"And what's the likelihood of that?"

"It's too early to tell. We'll have to see what evidence we can bring to bear."

"We'll do our level best, sir," Kate assured him.

"I know you will."

"They have the full weight of the NCA behind them, too," Damon assured him."

"Good, and Kate, I've discussed the events in Ireland with Damon, and given you were just a teenager at the time, and the circumstances of the event, we're quite certain we can make it go away. It won't affect your position here."

Kate blushed. "Thank you, sir."

"Besides, your work has been exemplary. I have no reason to discipline you for that."

"She'll never fit her head out of the door, Darrell," DCI Dean commented.

"Now, we wouldn't want that, would we?"

Kate shook her head.

"Now, I do have some other news for you. As you know, the Surry Constabulary has been reviewing whether to keep Horsley Station open, mainly due to budget cuts and unfortunately, it's been deemed too expensive to keep open."

"What?" Nathan asked.

The Chief raised his hand to forestall any further protests. "However, I have also received word from the National Crime Agency that they will be taking over the property and installing Damon and his team here permanently."

"So, what does that mean for us?" Nathan asked.

"It means you have a choice," the Chief answered. "You can move back to Mount Browne with the rest of us, or you can remain here and join Damon's Task Force."

Kate looked up at Nathan. He looked back at her and shrugged. "Well?"

"I want to stay," Kate replied.

"I do too," he agreed.

"Excellent," Kate exclaimed.

***

"It's been a crazy few days," Nathan said after pulling up outside Kate's flat.

"Yeah, it certainly has," Kate agreed.

"I hope you don't mind me saying, but you seem happier."

Kate smiled. "Yeah, I think I am. I don't think I was aware of how much crap I was just carrying around with me, you know? But now that Abban is behind bars, and my secret's out, all that weight is just gone."

"That's good to know," Nathan replied with a smile. "Our work is far from over, though."

"Oh, I know. I'll see you tomorrow, okay?"

"Yep, catch you later." Nathan winked at her. Kate got out and wandered up to her building and walked inside. The moment she stepped in through the door, Francine's front door opened.

"Hello, Kate," Francine greeted her.

"Hi, Francine. How are you today?" She was still sporting the bruising from her kidnapping, but it was good to see her up and about.

"Very well, thank you. Very well. You got him, didn't you? The police that came here to his flat said you got him."

Kate smiled. "We did. He's all locked up now. You don't need to worry."

"Good. That's good."

"Are you okay? Are you coping alright?"

Francine nodded. "I'll be fine. I get bad dreams sometimes, but yes, I'm okay."

"That's good. You look after yourself, and keep your door locked, okay?"

"I will," Francine replied, and retreated into her flat, locking the door behind her as Kate had suggested. Kate felt bad that Francine had gone through that ordeal. She wished there was something she could have done to prevent it. But at least she'd survived.

Returning to her room, Kate collapsed on her bed and for a long while, just lay there, letting the stresses of the day fade away and drain out of her.

For the first time in as long as she could remember, she had no feelings of dread or worry about what tomorrow would bring. The Black Hand was still out there, sure, they were still a threat, but Abban himself—at least for now—was out of the picture. She knew who he was, where he was, and also that he wasn't a direct threat to her anymore. He couldn't blackmail her or taunt her or hurt her, and that was a very freeing feeling.

After a while, Kate sat up and her eyes came to rest on a photo nearby of her aunt, Fiona.

Kate smiled. "We got him," she whispered. "Rest in peace Fi."

THE END

Author Note

Writing these thrillers has been an interesting experience and a compelling challenge for me as a writer. Before writing the first one, I hadn't been certain that I could pull off the kind of twisty-turny tale with a suitable sting in its telling that a crime thriller demanded, but crafting this series has been a fun and rewarding experience.

This book brings the series to an end, at least for the time being. I may return to it at some point, but for now, this book is the final chapter in Kate's story.

Initially, I put these books out under my Penname, A L Fraine, and while I will keep that name on the books, I've chosen to add my actual name to them as well. The main reason for this is because they are part of a wider universe of books that I publish under Andrew Dobell. That universe is called The Magi Saga, and a couple of characters from that wider universe appear in cameo roles in the later part of this book.

If books about Magic and weird and wonderful adventures are not your thing, then they might not be for you, but if you'd like to learn more about Amanda and Rebecca, then check out the links below.

Amanda's tale begins here:
www.amazon.com/dp/B081K2H74Y

Rebecca's is here:
www.amazon.com/dp/B07R8M84RK/

If you would like to connect with me more online, I have a Facebook Group where I'm very active.
You can find that here:
www.facebook.com/groups/MagiSagaFans/

Thank you so much for joining me on this thrilling journey.
Best Regards,
Andrew

Book List

The complete A L Fraine Book list:
www.alfraineauthor.co.uk

Printed in Great Britain
by Amazon